# Crisis in Uzbekistan

✳

CHARLES H. MYERS

Trafford
PUBLISHING™

Order this book online at www.trafford.com/07-2861
or email orders@trafford.com

Most Trafford titles are also available at major online book retailers.

Edited by: Susan Snowden

Printed in Victoria, BC, Canada.

ISBN: 978-1-4251-6259-7 (sc)
ISBN: 978-1-4269-9864-5 (dj)

*Our mission is to efficiently provide the world's finest, most comprehensive
book publishing service, enabling every author to experience success.
To find out how to publish your book, your way, and have it available
worldwide, visit us online at www.trafford.com/10510*

*Trafford rev. 11/9/2009*

www.trafford.com

North America & international
toll-free: 1 888 232 4444 (USA & Canada)
phone: 250 383 6864 ♦ fax: 812 355 4082

# Chapter One

The caravan had been cobbled together from many sources. It included old jeeps, military trucks of all types and ages, Humvees [mostly from the military advisers and legation], and various civilian vehicles including one motorcycle with a sidecar and an ambulance from the dark ages. Some of the vehicles were almost empty except for a few pieces of luggage, while others carried pieces of prized furniture that had been collected by some of the military families.

I rode in the cab of the tenth truck of our caravan traveling along a wide graveled road. It was a clear, cool October day, but there had been no rain for several days. Dust was everywhere. Even with the windows closed it seeped into the cab. It obscured the back of the vehicle ahead forcing the convoy to stretch out. Only the first vehicle had a clear view of the road. The rest of the convoy saw dust and sometimes the rear of the preceding vehicle. It was much like a dog team. Only the lead dog saw ahead. The rest of the team saw the rear of the dog in front of them.

This country was different from Bangor, Maine, where I had been practicing internal medicine with a group and was now on a six months sabbatical. Looking back, things had not been bad in Bangor compared with practicing medicine here, but after the rather prolonged malpractice suit I had felt the need to get away. Although I had been exonerated in the trial, I had felt depressed and wanted to try something different. Uzbekistan was different and interesting, but I missed my family. The reasons for the sabbatical didn't seem nearly as important as they had when I left.

I was working in a medical clinic in Radisgrad, Uzbekistan, when the rebel forces were sighted in the hills nearby. All the foreign volunteers on staff had been ordered to leave for their own safety. I had stayed behind for a day to organize the locals who would run the clinic in our absence. Dr. Brown and the foreign nurses had loaded their gear and left with the legation staff and other westerners from the area guarded by a large unit of military advisers. I was to leave with the Marines from the legation guard and any stragglers from the outlying missions. We had followed a little more than a day later and were hurrying to join the main group. We expected to join them later today or early tomorrow.

Radisgrad, which had been my home for the past

four and a half months, was a small farming commu-
nity with a clinic that passed as a hospital. The pharmacy across the street from the clinic provided most of
the medical supplies to the clinic as the clinic had few
medications of its own. When a patient was admitted,
a prescription for the medicine and supplies needed for
his or her care would be given to the family, who would
purchase the material at the pharmacy and bring it to
the clinic.

The clinic was a rectangular building with fifteen
beds at one end serving as the hospital. There was one
operating room and a nursing station. The remainder of
the building was examining rooms and office space. It
was functional but not particularly architecturally pleas-
ing. It was in the old Soviet style.

As we left Radisgrad, a group of Russian soldiers
under the command of Major Arinski joined our convoy.
They were not a unit but were from several different
units. Apparently, they had been separated from their
larger force, and they too were attempting to get back
to the main body. There were over two hundred of them
crammed into six Russian trucks with their weapons
and ammunition. We could offer them food and riding
space, and they offered us additional protection.

There was no unified command. Although Major
Arinski was the ranking officer and commanded the
larger force, a Marine lieutenant, James Anderson, was
making most of the decisions for the caravan. He was
young, inexperienced, and arrogant. The Russian major
was experienced and laid back, but he kept firm command of his forces.

I was riding with John Branson, an engineer for

Johnson Oil Company, and we had been together for the past two hours. The day before I rode with a teacher and his family, but they had stayed behind this morning with car trouble. It was expected they would join us this evening when we met the larger group of refugees ahead of us. John had taken me as he was riding alone and wanted company. Since I did not know anything about cars except how to drive one and would have been of little help to the family, I had accepted John's invitation. John was a large man with light brown hair down to his neck. He was wearing a brown wool shirt and a blue wool coat that opened around him. As we rode, he told me about himself. He had been born in Detroit, but his family had moved to New Orleans when his father graduated from law school and went to work for Johnson Oil. John had grown up in Louisiana and joined his father at Johnson Oil after graduating from college.

He had begun telling me about his childhood in New Orleans when the truck ahead of us suddenly loomed out of the dust. John jammed on the brakes, and we waited for the truck behind us to run up our rear. However, that did not occur. It seemed everyone was awake.

"Wait a moment while I try to find out what's going on," I told John as I opened the door and got out.

The dust was beginning to settle as I walked toward the front of the convoy. Several vehicles ahead a small group of civilians had already gathered and were listening to a Marine sergeant. I joined them.

"Just be patient," he said. "Lieutenant Anderson has sent a few scouts ahead to see what's over the next ridge. We'll be moving shortly and expect the legation force to be just ahead of us."

"Why do you need to scout ahead? Why not just drive over the ridge and see when we get there?" asked a woman in the crowd. I thought that was a good question.

"There was some firing and noise as we approached the ridge," the sergeant answered. "The lieutenant thought it would be prudent to investigate before we advanced further. We know there's a rebel force in the area, but we don't know where it is."

I had thought the rebel army under General Stratiscof was behind us and that was the reason we were forced to leave. How could he have gotten around us? Maybe all the reports were wrong, and he never was threatening our area. For modern times with satellites, planes, cell phones, etc., information was not very reliable here. After all, Stratiscof must have a large army, and I thought that would be easy to follow.

"Please wait in your vehicles," the sergeant requested. "It shouldn't be more than a few minutes."

The group broke up slowly. I returned to my truck and told John what I had learned.

He turned off the engine and said, "A few minutes can be a long time in the military. It's often hours if not days."

"Who knows," I said. "I don't know what he was talking about weapons firing either. I couldn't hear anything, but we were pretty far back from the ridge."

"What's everyone else doing?" he asked.

"Some of the people from the front vehicles were going up to the ridge, which isn't very high, but I couldn't see what they were doing up there. Others are just milling around, waiting."

"I guess we wait also."

"I suppose so. You were telling me about life growing up in New Orleans," I said. "Tell me more."

"Yeah. It was a great life for a kid," he said. "We weren't far from Lake Pontchartrain, and I loved fishing and swimming. One of my friends had an old rowboat that we used for fishing, and if we caught enough of the good-sized ones, we could usually talk one of our mothers into cooking them for us. Of course, we had to clean them first." He paused and then said, "I remember the summer evenings when it began to cool off. We would watch the sun go down over the tranquil lake. Sometimes there would be the wake of a boat, but otherwise the water was calm. The setting sun would reflect gold and white off the dark water. When there were clouds, they would turn red and then pink as the sun set until it was dark except for a glow in the western sky. It was a relaxed and peaceful lifestyle since we weren't involved in the tourist sections of town. Later I joined my father at Johnson Oil. He worked in the office but got me a summer job working on the rigs when I was in high school. It was hard work, but for a kid it was fun, and there was a good deal of camaraderie. I went to work for them full time later.

"After my dad died suddenly of a heart attack, my mother moved back to Detroit to be near her family. She has a sister and an aunt living in Hamtramck. I continued to work for Johnson but was in Texas when Katrina hit and destroyed New Orleans. I guess we were lucky to have left before the storm although we had friends who lost their homes. When Johnson became involved in Russian oil, they shipped me here to work on building the oil line. I've been here for a few months now, but I'd like to get back to the States."

"Are you married?" I asked.

"No, I have a few girl friends but nothing serious. My plan is to settle on a small farm in the Midwest with a wife and a couple of children. Constantly moving is fun for a while. You meet new people and see different areas, but it gets old quickly."

"Where did you go to college?"

"I studied engineering at LSU before I went to work for Johnson Oil full time," he replied and then pointed toward the ridge. "Everyone's coming back in a hurry. Something's happening."

Before I could reply, the lead jeep went past us going the way we had just come. A second jeep followed stopping at each vehicle. When it got to us, the sergeant simply told us to turn around and follow them. No other news or explanation was given, but I guessed we would learn soon enough the why and where.

I could see the trucks in front of us backing up and turning to go back. All of the people who had gone up to the ridge were hustling into the vehicles.

John started the engine without comment and pulled ahead to turn around. As we were turning, a man carrying cameras and what appeared to be photographic equipment over his shoulders stopped us and asked for a ride. He was a small, clean-shaven man wearing a blue jacket and pants and heavy boots. Like the rest of us, he was covered with dust

"There's plenty of room in the rear. Help yourself,"

John told him.

He put his equipment in the back of the truck and jumped in. Again we started down the road following the column through the dust.

After a few miles of riding in silence, we were forced to stop once more. John leaned forward on the steering wheel, stretched his shoulders, and said, "I suspect that it wasn't good news on the other side of that ridge. It must've been part of the rebel force. I wonder if the refugees ahead of us got through."

"It could have been anything. We didn't get much information," I replied.

"What else would make us turn around and hustle out of there? I guess we'll have to wait on the rebel forces to move on before we can proceed. That means it will take us awhile to catch up to our main group."

"Who knows, John? If you're right, we'll need to hide out for some time where the rebel forces won't find us, and I don't know where that would be."

"The rebels will probably move through quickly," he replied. "Oh! It looks like we're moving again."

As I looked up, the door next to me opened and our passenger asked me to move over. I slid over, and he climbed in next to me.

"Thanks," he said. "My name is Roger Taylor. I appreciate the ride, but it's lonely riding in the back. The truck I was riding in left without me. I guess I stayed too long on the ridge, but I was trying to get as many pictures as I could to send back to the station."

"You work for a newspaper?" I asked.

"No, I work for CNN and was covering the war from the legation when it was evacuated. It seemed like a good time to leave, but I waited to leave with the last of the staff."

"What was happening on the other side of the ridge?" John asked, "We left in a hurry and were given no information."

"Yeah. We initially heard gunfire and Lieutenant Anderson, who seems to be in charge, decided to investigate before we got too close. Everyone from the first few vehicles walked up to the ridge, but I don't think anyone expected to see what we saw. Our main group was in the valley about a half mile away and the rebel forces, most of which were further down the valley, surrounded them. There were a couple of thousand mingling with the convoy and were firing shots into the air. It took a couple of minutes for me to realize that they were not just firing into the air but were killing our people. When I used my long distance lens, I could see that they were not only killing them but were assaulting them as well. I set up my TV camera, shot footage of the whole thing, and sent it back to headquarters. I also shot some still photos, which I still have. They are gruesome, but I'll show them to you if you like. They'll give you some idea of what was happening."

"Sure," I said. "I didn't know you could send TV pictures from here."

"Modern satellite communication is wonderful. The pictures take a few minutes, but the text goes quickly. All the stuff I sent this afternoon is probably on the air already. Here are some of the stills I took." He handed me the photos, which were indeed graphic and detailed. They appeared to have been taken from a few feet away.

Before I had a chance to look at more than the first two, we turned right onto a smaller road heading toward the mountains. I did not think we would get very far down this road as we were already at the base of the mountains. On our left was a vodka brewing company, according to the sign, and an even smaller paved road led to the front of the plant. An old open-back truck sat, apparently abandoned, at the intersection of the two roads. The fields between the factory and our road were flat and covered with high grasses. A few trees surrounded the plant, which seemed to be about a quarter mile away.

"Turn up that road, John, and let's see if there are any free samples at that plant," I said.

"I didn't realize you were a heavy drinker, Doc,"John said as he turned left. "Then again, I haven't known you very long, have I?"

"I've been known to have a drink every now and then, but I'm hoping we can find a few cases of vodka and move them to that abandoned truck. If the rebels saw us and try to follow us, they might be tempted to stop for a few drinks rather than rush after us."

"I doubt it. Professional soldiers aren't going to be detoured by some vodka. They'll ignore it," Roger said.

"Yes, I know, but most of the rebel forces aren't trained soldiers. If the rumors are true that they're untrained militia, some free booze might distract them. Besides, it can't hurt, and it might slow them down a bit," I replied.

"No, it won't hurt, and it might be interesting to see what this plant looks like," Roger said. "However, I don't think the rebels noticed us up on the ridge. They were too busy killing and raping to notice much of anything, and no one was guarding the ridge. The whole nightmare seemed disorganized and out of control. If Stratiscof is in control of his army, he'll move them toward the main battle site. If they come after us, then Stratiscof can't control them, and they'll kill all of us as well."

"We might lose our choice of camping sites," John commented as he drove us toward the plant.

At the end of the driveway, we turned into a loading area and pulled up to the dock. The plant was surprisingly modern appearing and quite large. The building was white cinderblock with a green metal roof, and it was well maintained. They must have been doing very good business as paved roads led to the office and the loading dock. Even the parking lot was nicely landscaped.

A lone truck was backed up to the loading dock. The parking lot was otherwise deserted, and no one came to greet us.

"We're here. Let's see what we can find," John said, and we all got out. I climbed onto the loading dock and tried the large roll-up doors, but they were locked.

Roger had more success with the back of the truck, which was half full of boxes marked Vodka. He tore open one of the boxes. "Bingo!" he said. "These all appear to be loaded with vodka. They must've departed in some hurry to leave this truck half full of bottles. However, it is convenient for us. We can drive the truck out to the road and leave it."

"No, I'd like to put a few cases on the old truck where they can be seen but leave the rest here. If they can see the booze, they are more likely to be attracted to it and come down to the plant. That could buy us some time. We can put the cases in our truck and unload them on the open-back truck," I told them.

"They'll know from the sign that this is a vodka plant. Even those who can't read will recognize the word vodka," John pointed out.

"True," I replied, "but seeing the product is a big stimulus."

"All right," Roger said. "If you and John will get some of the cases loaded on the truck, I'll take some pictures to send to the station. Maybe you'll be on the evening news."

As Roger went to get his equipment, John went to inspect the rest of the building, and I began moving the cases of vodka to the back of our truck.

In a few minutes John returned and told us that the rest of the doors were locked as well. However, I didn't think that would be a problem for a bunch of booze hungry men.

John and I finished loading eight cases onto our truck while Roger shot his footage. When he finished, Roger put his camera in and closed the back of the truck.

As John drove us back toward the intersection, I asked Roger why he wanted pictures of the plant.

"When you're presenting the news, you can't just have someone sit and read it. That would be very boring. It's much more interesting to have pictures from the activity or the area to show while the news is being presented. I'll also do shots of the mountains and the river behind us as background. For radio you don't need any of that."

"That makes sense," I said. "Where's the river? I didn't see it."

"It's just to the other side of the plant. It must start up in the mountains and probably formed this valley. I'm sure that it's the water supply for this plant."

John pulled up next to the abandoned truck and said, "Let's move this stuff and get on down the road. Our convoy has gone, and I don't like being out here by ourselves."

"Don't worry, John. I don't see any sign of anyone coming, and I doubt they even know we're here," Roger told him.

Unfortunately, that turned out to be wrong.

# Chapter Two

It was a beautiful evening with mild temperatures and a crispness to the air that suggested that winter was not far away. As we had come over the dusty plain, the lower hills covered with green trees could be seen with the hazy gray mountain peaks behind them. Some of the mountains had a skim of white on them, much like frosting on a roll. It lifted everyone's spirits after traveling for several days across the flat, brown landscape with only a few rolling hills to break the monotony. The few trees were along the banks of the rivers or streams. We had seen some scattered herds of cattle, and the people in the occasional village appeared poor and downtrodden. The children playing in the dirt along the side of the road we were traveling were round-faced and poorly clothed. The houses were small wooden structures with few windows. In contrast to the primitive conditions around us our convoy had plenty of vehicles, food, and, of course, armament. There had been time to gather the essentials before fleeing two days ago and there had been opportunities to restock gas and food along the way.

Although I lived in the mountains in Maine, these mountains were different. Maine's mountains are mostly smaller, rounded, and covered with hardwood trees with flamboyant leaves in the fall. True, Mount Katahdin, the tallest peak in Maine, is all rock, but it is not steep or tall, being about five thousand two hundred feet. Here the peaks were sharp, steep, and over nine or ten thousand feet. The lower portions were covered with evergreens and a few scattered hardwoods, but the higher elevations were rugged and bare of foliage.

Rivers and streams formed valleys, and the plains appeared fertile and were forested except where they had been cleared for grazing or farming. The whole area had a rustic beauty and peacefulness and in some ways seemed idyllic. However, the flies, gnats, and mosquitoes swarmed everywhere as a reminder that this was real life and not a movie.

The main road we had traveled was in one of the plains formed by a river and lined by the mountain ranges. This side road was unpaved and led into a long, flat valley. With the exception of the vodka distilling facility at the start of the road, I had not seen any houses or other buildings as we drove along the valley floor.

At this point I guessed the valley was over a mile

wide with a small river in the center. Although the valley had run straight for several miles, it turned to form an S-shaped curve here. Behind me it apparently ended in a narrow ravine with steep cliffs on both sides a half mile further. Our chance of escape was limited by the geography. I suspect this fact was unknown to the command when they led us up this side road in an attempt to avoid the army now camping on the long, sloping hillside across from where I sat.

The river was not deep and only a few feet wide this time of year, really not much more than a stream, and the dirt road crossed it by a ford in the middle of the valley. On this side of the valley was a quarter-mile gently rising wooded hillside ending in a gray rock wall. On either side of the clear, rock-strewn stream the flat area had been cleared and was covered in brown grass. Upstream the river curved to the left and disappeared into the rapidly narrowing ravine, and in the opposite direction it flowed relatively straight to the larger river about two miles distance. The road was on the left of the stream and hugged the valley wall. The valley in that direction had been cleared of trees to allow foraging of cattle and sheep. No animals were present now.

Across from the small rock on which I sat the hill ended in a steep rock promontory on which rockets or mortars were being placed. The rest of the area on both sides of the river was covered with men moving like worker ants building fires for cooking and setting up sleeping areas. To the right of the river was more military activity with foxholes and trenches being prepared and guns placed. Otherwise it was peaceful with a clear blue sky interrupted by an occasional cloud, and this late in the afternoon the sun did not reach the valley floor.

Our group was mostly in the pine trees that covered the slope, but there was some military activity beyond the tree line. All of us were fleeing the violence caused by the rebels who declared that they were patriots fighting for independence. Of our group two hundred and nineteen were the Russian soldiers who had joined our flight earlier in the day, forty-four were American Marines or soldiers who had served as legation guards, and fifty-two were civilians. Of the civilians some were American military family members, others were administrative personnel, but most were missionary teachers or medical personnel of whom I was one, and there were two tourists.

Across from us was a rebel force made up of twenty thousand men gathered from militia and two tribes in the region. A "General" Stratiscof commanded the force. Bringing these tribal fighters together had been a major coup for Stratiscof since the enmity between them had been present for generations, and its origin had long since been forgotten. The militia had some training and discipline, but the rest were an armed rabble. However, twenty thousand armed men was an impressive force to add to the rebel army fighting to the north of us and would give General Stratiscof considerable influence among the rebel leaders.

Despite the noise and activity I heard someone approaching behind me. As I turned in that direction I saw a young woman wearing dark blue pants, black boots, and a heavy brown jacket emerge from the trees. She was probably in her twenties, fair with long blond hair and no makeup, which was not surprising considering our situation. When she saw me, she walked over in my direction.

"Hi," she said as she looked across the valley. "Aren't you worried about being so exposed to view?"

"I doubt they're looking to shoot us this evening since we're in their grasp. They can do what they want with us in the morning," I replied.

"What a comforting thought!" she said as she sat down next to me and put her arms about her knees.

"I'm Robert Jacoby," I told her. "Who are you and what brought you to this area of the world? It isn't exactly a tourist mecca."

"No it isn't, but it is spectacular in a rugged and impressive way. Look at those mountains. This would be a lovely valley under other circumstances." She paused and then said, "My name is Dorothy Roberts, and I'm twenty-five years old. I grew up in a small Texas town, which you probably don't know. My father was a Baptist preacher there. It was a nice town, and I knew many of the people, but there wasn't much to do. I left and went to Greenville, South Carolina, to study education. Then I came here as a Christian missionary and to teach elementary school children.

"It's always been a dream of mine to travel and live in other parts of the world. When the church offered me the opportunity to work in this area of Russia for a couple of years, I volunteered without a second thought. I learned the language from a Russian family that I lived with, but I don't speak it very well. Working with the children has been fun. They were mostly eager to learn and had so little compared to Americans. I felt as if I was accomplishing something worthwhile. What about you? Is your family with you?"

"I volunteered to work for six months in the clinic in Radisgrad, a small town about twenty-five miles west of here. I left my family home in Maine. When the rebellion began a month ago, I should have left with many of the others of the staff, but there was so much to be done. I guess I didn't believe the rebels would bother with us."

I know," she said. "The school was so isolated and the area so backward I thought no one would be interested in us. What would they hope to gain? Why not go fight the main army and take over the cities where the power and money are? It still doesn't make much sense to me."

"It seems to be a matter of power and forcing men to join them," I said. "General Stratiscof has gathered an impressive force, mostly from two tribes who've hated each other for centuries. The groups seem to have nothing in common except for a dislike for the Russian government and Westerners. He has twenty thousand or so men and is still recruiting."

"He's an ogre and scares me to death. Look at what he did to the people ahead of us who included staff from several consulates and aid missions. That was awful. And now we're facing the same fate."

"Yeah, I know. Did you see what happened today?" I asked.

"I saw quite a bit," she replied. "One of the missionaries with me had binoculars, and he let me look for a few minutes. It was terrible."

"I didn't go to the ridge, but I had a good look at the pictures taken by Roger, the CNN reporter. They were graphic and with his equipment appeared to be taken up close. He sent all of them to his office, but I can't imagine them being published or shown on television. They were too gruesome, which might sell papers, but I would think there would be complaints about the graphic horror and the invasion of privacy of those dying. What did you see?"

"You saw the pictures. They give a pretty good idea of what went on."

"I know," I replied. "I wondered if you saw the same things."

"Well," Dorothy said. "I was in the third truck behind the Humvee carrying Lieutenant Anderson. When I first heard the gunfire, I thought it was thunder in the distance, but it was continuous and became louder as we approached, and we realized it was gunfire. When we came to the last little hill before the next village, we stopped, and Lieutenant Anderson got out and walked up the road with several Marines. All of us followed them. At the top of the rise the Marines went off into the tall grass on one side of the road and into the trees on the other. Mr. Thacker, our pastor, and I went to the right and lay down in the grass. He took out his binoculars and searched the road in front of us. The road curved toward the right and down the hill where there were a few houses. All the open fields and the village were covered with people and vehicles. The convoy we were to join was stopped in the village. I couldn't tell much from watching, but Mr. Thacker gasped and moaned before putting down the glasses. I asked if I could look, and he told me no, that it was too horrible.

"Since I was curious, I insisted, and he finally handed

me the binoculars. At first when I looked, I couldn't tell what was happening, but then I saw Mrs. Harris. Her dress was up, and there was a man raping her. I could see the pain and terror on her face. Just then he finished and rammed his knife in between her legs. I saw her scream but couldn't hear her. Mr. Harris was on the other side of her and was held by two men. His face was bloody, and his pants were down. He was being sodomized while his wife was raped. I looked beyond the Harrises and saw a little child screaming and being held up with a bayonet through his abdomen with his arms and legs flailing. I couldn't look any more. I don't know how Roger could stand to take all the pictures he did."

"That's awful. What did you do then?"

"I was sick, and then we went back to our truck."

"How many others witnessed what you saw?"

"Maybe three or four. I don't know," she replied.

"Those deaths were painful and inhuman," I said. "I'm sorry that you had to see them."

"But what about us? What about the women and children? Don't we face the same thing?" she asked. "I'm glad I don't have family here."

I didn't know any answer to that question. Looking across the valley there seemed to be endless masses of men like bees swarming over a hive. My military experience had been as an enlisted man working in a headquarters company after the Vietnam War and before I went to medical school. Not an ideal preparation for this situation. It seemed to me we needed a major air strike followed by five thousand or more special force troops to rescue us. I would accept American, Russian, or anybody. But as near as I could tell, none appeared likely to come. I hoped that Lieutenant Anderson or Major Arinski had a better plan or at least some plan. The pictures showed the fear and horror on the faces of the victims as they faced the madness of rape, torture, and pain this afternoon. Death must have come as a relief. As a doctor I had seen death a number of times, but I did not relish facing that kind of demise.

"I don't know. The world is aware of our situation since Roger has documented what happened for everyone to see," I replied. "Someone somewhere must have an idea of how to rescue us. America has fleets and planes around the world. We're the most powerful nation on the earth. I would hope they could come for us. What's the rest of the group saying?"

"No one knows what's going on. Lieutenant Anderson hasn't told us a word. Most of the information we have is from the news reports on the radio, and those are mainly what we already know. The torture and massacre of the refugees ahead of us is the big news. I think that the civilians are planning to have a meeting since we are not included in any decisions that are being made by Lieutenant Anderson and Major Arinski."

"When is that to take place?" I asked.

"I don't know. No time was set the last I heard. Most people are setting up shelters or preparing food for tonight, and the mothers are busy taking care of their children. Everyone wants to have a part in the decisions and know what's going to happen. This is particularly true for the families. I'm single and don't have the increased burden of worrying about children. Still I would like to be there for the meeting since we're all trapped.

Have you spoken to your wife recently?"

"Unfortunately I was unable to contact her before we left since my cell phone chose this time to quit. She doesn't know where I am, but maybe that's just as well under the circumstances. Anyway, I was enjoying a little time to myself and thinking about my family."

"I'm sorry I interrupted you," Dorothy said.

"No, I'm glad you came. I haven't met many people in our group, and it's nice to have someone to talk to."

She stood and gazed across the valley. She was an attractive woman, and I wondered why she had not married.

She must have read my thoughts because she said, "I've always wanted children of my own but haven't met the right man. Now I wonder if I'll have the chance to have a family. Sometimes you think there's plenty of time, and there should be no rush to marry. But you never know how much time you have. Life went on while I was still making plans."

"Don't worry. You'll have plenty of opportunities. I'm sure we'll all get through this," I replied. "Let's walk back to the camp area and see if there's any news."

"I certainly hope that you're right. It just doesn't look very promising now."

I stood and brushed off my pants as she started over the rocks toward the main camp. I followed her. We turned toward the trees to our right, and as we walked into the shade of the tall pine trees, the air became cooler. The pine needles crunched under our boots, but the walking was fairly easy as there was little undergrowth.

It was becoming dark quickly. Several small fires

had been started in scooped out areas, and blankets and bedrolls were scattered in small groups. Most of the people were up to our right in a semi-open area. Dorothy turned and climbed up the hill to join them. I went with her.

Some of the younger children were playing on the scattered rocks but most were just sitting watching the adults. One young man with bushy black hair and dressed in dark jeans and an open jacket was speaking on a cell phone. Most cell phones had lost power awhile back. Everyone was tired. Most of the adults were listening to the small battery-operated radio that a gray-haired man dressed in boots, blue jeans, and a wool shirt was holding. There were thirty or more people surrounding him, and all had on whatever warm clothing they could find. Mismatched but warm was the fashion of the day.

Dorothy went to speak to a woman feeding her young children, and I joined the circle around the radio.

"What's happening?" I asked a man standing along the back of the crowd.

"The president has been assured by General Stratiscof that we'll be freed in the morning and that he has no intention of harming us. The president has ordered the Marines to surrender," he replied.

"And us along with them, I presume."

"Yeah, I presume," he replied.

# CHAPTER THREE

Joy Jacoby was five foot three inches tall; slim, with gray eyes, full lips and straight dark hair that she wore down to her shoulders. She had a petite figure, which she had worked to keep after the birth of her one child, and today she was wearing a short, light blue knit dress that flattered her figure and contrasted with her hair. She was almost thirty-two years old, and she and Robert had been married for ten years. They married in his second year of medical school at Tufts in Boston, and she had worked as a secretary to help support them while he completed school. She retired when she became pregnant, and Robert provided for them during his internship and residency with help from a small inheritance from his parents, both of whom had died before she met Robert.

It was almost eight in the morning as Joy got her son, Bobby, into his jacket and backpack for school. Bobby was eight years old and, like most kids his age, was not a morning person on school days. On weekends he was up early to watch cartoons, but weekdays were another story.

"Hurry up, Bobby. You're going to miss your bus," she said as she handed him his lunch box.

"Don't worry, Mom. I have plenty of time. The bus always runs late."

Joy bent down and kissed him on the forehead and finally got him out the door with his lunch box in hand. She watched from the porch as he ambled slowly toward the tree-lined sidewalk and turned left for the corner where he would catch the school bus.

Before going back inside she noted that the maple leaves were beginning to turn to their autumn colors of red and yellow. The sky was a clear deep blue, and the air was cool and crisp. It was definitely fall. As she turned to go back into the two-story white clapboard house that they had purchased three years ago, she saw her neighbor, Janet, waving to her and starting across the yard. Janet wore a brown sweater, and Joy wished she had put on a sweater or jacket before coming outside. However, she closed the door and went to meet Janet.

"Good morning," Joy said.

"Hi," Janet replied. Janet was in her early fifties with gray hair that she kept in a helmet cut, the fashion of the day for women of her age. She had a pleasant face with forehead wrinkles and crow's-feet around her eyes. She was large busted and slightly over weight, but she appeared heavier in the bulky sweater she was wearing.

"Would you like to come in for coffee?" Joy asked. "I have a fresh pot brewing."

"Thanks, but I can only stay a few minutes. Have you heard the news this morning?"

"No. I've been getting Bobby fed and off to school. That takes a regiment," Joy replied.

"Isn't Robert in southern Russia?" Janet asked.

"Well, he's in Uzbekistan, and I expect him back next month."

"According to the television there is some sort of rebellion going on in the mountains there. The rebels killed a bunch of refugees including some Americans yesterday and have another group trapped in a valley. It was on the morning news," Janet said.

"I haven't heard anything about it. I know there's a battle going on, but I thought it was a long way from where Robert is."

Joy led the way into the small kitchen that was painted white with a cornice of multicolored fruits and flowers. The cabinets were brown oak with white knobs, and the countertops were done in dark blue Formica with gray flecks.

She brought two mugs of coffee to the small table in front of the window and turned on the television, which sat on a stand next to the table.

"You take yours black, don't you?" Joy asked.

"Yes, thank you. What have you heard from Robert?"

Joy considered and said, "I heard from him a couple

of days ago, and he didn't think that they'd be bothered by the rebels since they were fairly isolated. He did say they were prepared to evacuate if there was any threat. Let's see if we can get some news now."

Joy switched the channel to CNN where the woman was pointing to a map of southern Russia and Uzbekistan indicating where the fighting was taking place.

"This is the area where Russian troops and their allies are facing a large and well-equipped rebel force," the newswoman was saying. "There's another rebel force under General Stratiscof made up of twenty thousand troops moving to join the main rebel force. General Stratiscof's contingent is composed mainly of local tribes and is the group that brutally killed the refugees yesterday. This force has apparently followed a second group of Westerners who were trying to escape the war and has trapped them in a small valley.

"We have spoken to Mark Nevin, a retired army colonel last stationed in Moscow and now senior adviser to Senator Morris, regarding the developments in Uzbekistan," the newswoman said. "He spoke to us earlier by phone.

"Mr. Nevin, could you give us a brief summary of what has been happening in this fight and your opinion of the current situation?"

"Certainly, Margaret. As you know, a group of rebels calling themselves Liberationists have been gathering troops and equipment for some time. They are trying to overthrow the Russian influenced government as they have a different religion and ethnic background. The only thing these small tribes have in common is their dislike for the Russians. After a number of years of terrorist activity, they've put together an army of young men taken from all the tribes and equipped them using foreign money. These men have had training from dissident Russian military officers and now are moving toward Russia.

"General Stratiscof, who has been recruiting more rebels, has about five thousand of these troops and fifteen thousand armed tribesmen. He was moving to join the other troops when he detoured into the Kakoura river valley to attack the Western refugees being displaced by the fighting. Why Stratiscof has done this is unclear. It is not to his advantage to antagonize Westerners or to waste time getting to the area where the main fighting is taking place."

"Why do you think he's done this? The attack on the refugees yesterday was brutal."

"He claims that he wasn't present at the time and that it was a small number of men who committed this act, Margaret. He says that they've all been executed. However, I have heard that we have pictures showing him present during the attack. I haven't seen the pictures and can't comment on them, but I understand a CNN reporter with a smaller group of refugees took them. Also, it would have taken a number of men to carry out the attack on fifteen hundred people, even if many were civilians."

"So you believe he ordered these attacks?"

"I don't know, Margaret. It doesn't make any sense unless he's sending a warning to not intervene or this is what will happen. We saw it with the beheadings in Iraq, although the rape and torture here is much worse if that's possible. We'll learn more when we see how he treats this second group of people. This group has a number of Russian troops and Marines in it."

"Where did these soldiers come from? I didn't know that there were any American Marines in the area, Mr. Nevin."

"Well, there are only about thirty or forty Marines who were part of an advisory and training force. The larger part of the American force was killed yesterday. This group was left behind to clean up and bring out some of the equipment. It was expected that they would rejoin the larger group today. The Russians are remnants of forces sent to fight the insurgents. There were several small engagements, and these men were either sepa-rated from their units or their units were destroyed. They had been gathered under Major Arinski and joined the Marines and the civilians a day or so ago. They are try-ing to rejoin their army and were moving with the refu-gees for the protection in numbers."

"Who's in command of this collection of troops?"

"Major Arinski is the ranking officer and the Marines are under the command of Lieutenant Anderson. There's no formal chain of command. However, the group is well supplied. There is the food, weapons, and ammunition that the Marines had plus the equipment the Russians brought," commented Mr. Nevin.

"What, in your opinion, will happen to this last group?"

"Margaret, it's difficult to know. Since General Stratiscof has followed them into a narrow ravine off the main road, I would guess that he's planning to at-tack them or hold them hostage, but why he would want to do that is unknown. There seems to be no reason to pursue them except to hold or kill them. They are no threat to him, and his army is needed at the battle. Even to capture three hundred or so people would not require his whole force. It's hard to understand."

"With the Russian soldiers and the Marine force, both of which you say are well-equipped, would they be able to hold off the rebel force until aid arrives?"

"I don't know the terrain in the area, but it would seem unlikely that a force of three hundred could hold such a large army at bay. Even if the valley that they're in is narrow so that only a few of the rebel troops could attack their front, the defenders still could be hit with cannon or mortar fire until their position was weakened enough to attack. This would be particularly true if the rebels held some high ground and could fire down on them. I would think that the terrain would have to be very favorable for the American and Russian force to hold out even briefly, and since neither Russia nor the U.S. have any forces available in the area, rescue is unlikely."

"Why didn't we get our people out before the rebels could attack them? Was there no warning of rebel forces in the area?"

"I don't think anyone anticipated that the rebels would attack Westerners, and most intelligence indicated that Stratiscof would move as quickly as possible to join other rebel forces in the north where fighting is already occurring. As soon as it appeared that the Stratiscof force was moving into the area, evacuation was ordered. However, it takes time to evacuate. It's not just a matter of jumping in the car and leaving. You have to warn the other Americans in the area, and these include a number of scattered missionaries, teachers and medical personnel as well as travelers. It all takes time, particularly in a rural area."

"Thank you for your insights, Mr. Nevin. We now return to our news desk."

Joy turned off the television and sipped her coffee.

"I really don't know where Robert is," Joy said. "I've tried to reach him by cell phone, but reception there is problematic at best."

"I'm sure he's fine, Joy, but I can understand that you would be worried about him. I have the bridge club this afternoon, so I must get back home. I did want to be sure that you knew what was happening where Robert is. If there's anything I can do for you, please let me know."

You really wanted to know if there was any gossip on Robert. Maybe he was mauled and murdered, and you could get some of the gory details for the bridge club today, Joy thought, but she only said "Thanks." She stood and followed Janet to the door. After Janet left, Joy waved good-bye and closed the door.

She cleared the two coffee cups from the table and placed them in the sink. She was worried about Robert, but there wasn't much she could do to help him. She needed to make the beds and do some grocery shopping. There never seemed to be much time before Bobby was home from school. When she went to school, the day seemed long, but as a mother with a child in school, the school day was always too short.

# CHAPTER FOUR

I moved through the circle of people toward the center trying to hear what was being said. A tall man wearing a heavy, dark blue overcoat that extended to his knees, battered brown boots, and a wool stocking cap was speaking loudly to the crowd. Although I could not see him well, I recognized the outfit as belonging to John Branson.

"We can't just give up to that bunch of murderers," he was saying. "You saw what happened to the group ahead of us this afternoon. Why would it be different for us? They sexually assaulted not only the women but the men as well. They used rifles and knives and clubs in the attack. It was brutal, and we can expect the same. I would rather be shot than face that kind of death."

A young woman who was wearing a short, dingy coat and long pants was holding a crying small child in a blanket. Her face was young and pale. She stood and spoke softly in a high-pitched voice. She was obviously terrified, and I suspected that many of the other people were also. The man next to her sat with his head in his hands.

"What are we to do? I don't want my child killed, and I don't want to die like that. We must follow the president's order and hope for the best," she said. "Look at all those men over there. How can we fight them? It would be crazy. We can't fight them with women and children."

A middle-aged woman stood and asked, "Why would the general want to hurt us? We are mostly volunteers helping the people in his country, and he needs us and the money we bring."

John Branson answered, "I don't know, but General Stratiscof was there this afternoon. The pictures showed him. How can the president not know that? He must have seen the pictures."

Another man stepped out from the crowd. "My name is Henry Jackson," he said. "I've been a teacher and missionary here for over ten years, and I can tell you that these young people live a hard life. Fighting and killing is a regular part of their existence, and the rest of life is routine and monotonous. They're eager for the excitement and the chance to get away from the tedious work. They have no discipline, and when they're worked up, their officers may not be able to control them. Why else would the whole force be here? Their leader's object is to join the rest of the rebel force. No matter what Stratiscof's plan, they don't need twenty thousand troops to capture three hundred of us."

A slim older woman with shoulder-length gray hair and dressed in a dark silver colored coat trimmed in fur at the neck and extending below her knees stepped into the center of the clearing. "I am Lily Blackthorne," she said. "Like many of you I am a volunteer. I have no children with me, but I can sympathize with the mothers who do. It would appear to me that Mr. Jackson is correct that Stratiscof is unable to control the majority of his troops. No other explanation makes sense. Also, it doesn't make sense for us to surrender. No matter what he promised the president, he's unlikely to have any better control of his army tomorrow than he had this afternoon. The question is what options are there for us. There are about two hundred Russian troops and forty American Marines against thousands of insurgents. The odds are not much improved even if the adult civilians join in the defense."

John spoke again. "If we're going to surrender, the Russian force will leave tonight. They have a mountaineering group with them and will try to get up into the mountain range behind us. They know what sort of treatment they'll get from the rebels."

"Why don't they take us with them?" asked another woman.

"They may not be able to make it even though they're trained troops. The way would be through snow-covered mountains for many days. They would never be able to take women and children on that sort of trip," he answered.

"But what alternatives do we have?" Lily asked. "We can't escape into the mountains, and I'm sure they'll not allow us to go back the way we came. If we surrender, we face the same horror that we saw this afternoon; I don't see how we can defend ourselves without outside help, which doesn't seem to be coming."

I thought about it for a moment and realized that Lily Blackthorne was right. The rebel troops were planning the same fate for us as they had administered to the group ahead of us. They were not in this fight for idealism or money. This was an adventure for them with rape and plunder as icing on the cake. Most of them were not disciplined or trained. They were more of an armed mob. There was no love lost between these groups, who would be just as happy to kill each other as us, but they were unified by the desire to kill and rape.

As I thought about the encampment across the valley, an idea occurred to me. But who would listen to me? I'm not a leader of men, and even if I talked to Lieutenant Anderson or Major Arinski, they wouldn't listen to me. Lieutenant Anderson was a young, inexperienced Marine officer who would not buck presidential orders. Also there was the problem of leaks to the enemy, who appeared to know all about our activities.

My opinions had not always been right in the past. I had lost at least one patient from making the wrong decision. I had been diligent and careful, I thought, but things had not turned out right despite that. Was my plan any better here? Maybe I should let someone else take the lead. I certainly wasn't infallible. On the other hand no one else seemed to have a workable plan or any plan for that matter, and it seemed better to try something than to be killed like rats in a trap. Someone needs to lead, I thought, but why should it be me?

"There might be a way," I said quietly to Lily.

"Who are you?" she asked.

"I am Robert Jacoby," I replied. "I'm a doctor and was working in a hospital as a volunteer. I agree that we're in danger, and I might have an idea to give us a chance. But everyone would have to help."

Lily came near to me. "Do you have any military experience?" she asked.

My military experience was mostly playing with metal soldiers when I was a kid. My friend, George, and I built roads in the dirt around trees and rocks in his backyard. The geography was not all that much different than where we were. It was largely pine trees, dirt, and rocks. In our game there was no military planning. The "enemy" attacked, and we would get pushed back to our base before we defeated them. There was no strategy, just explosions of dust and pine needles. The nice thing was that the Americans always won in the end.

"No," I replied. "However, this plan doesn't require military experience, but it does require secrecy. I'm afraid that Lieutenant Anderson will feel it's his duty to follow his commander's orders to surrender despite the obvious outcome. In that case the Russians will leave. I can probably get the Russians to stay and fight, but I may have to take over for Lieutenant Anderson. For that I would need the help of all the civilians. Lieutenant Anderson would have to know that we would not go along with surrendering and would fight him if he tried to force us."

"What's your idea, Robert?" John asked.

"I can't tell you now as it's essential that the plan doesn't reach the ears of the rebels."

"And why should we trust you?" Lily asked.

"I know," I said. "Think about this. How did the rebels even know that we were here? How did they know to pursue us down this road where we were hiding? I don't think they were aware of our presence when they attacked the people ahead of us. The only way they could learn of our movements is from us because no one else knew."

"I can't believe someone is telling them," she said.

"Nevertheless, they knew. I want to keep this plan as secret as possible for now. I'll need all the civilians to back me by being armed and keeping all our soldiers away. That might mean killing some, but that's not likely. We must appear as a unit prepared to fight."

"As you know, we were armed in preparation for an attack this afternoon," added John Branson. "Whether we can get everyone to support you is another question."

Jackson said, "If we're to have any say in the decision, we'll have to act as a group and agree on what we want to do. We'll need a leader to represent us to the military, and we'll need to support him or her. Otherwise, we will be slaughtered when we're handed over to the rebels as the president has ordered."

"The first thing is, do we all agree that surrender is the wrong thing to do?" Lily asked.

Most of the civilians were gathering around Lily. There were a few women caring for their children, and some people were wandering. A woman with a bundled-up child in her arms and another young boy next to her admitted that she was afraid for her children. Her husband had been with the group ahead of us, and she had expected to join him.

Another woman standing next to her husband asked who John was and why the American army couldn't rescue us or at least send the air force to free us. After all America is a super power, she pointed out.

John turned to her and said, "I'm John Branson, and I work for Johnson Oil Company. I'm here on business regarding the oil pipeline proposed for this area if peace can be established. In answer to your other question America is not a super power that can take on the world's troubles. We have enough problems trying to protect ourselves. There are no forces available to rescue us since our military is spread too thin, and they couldn't get here in time anyway. There are planes that could pick us up but not enough to fight the size army facing us. This is the reason the president has been forced to agree to turn us over to the rebels. The Russians don't have a force to send either as they're occupied with the other rebel army north of us."

"Well, what can we do?" asked another man. "We can't fight all those men."

"We can put up a good defense and try to discourage them from continuing to attack us. We are of no military or strategic significance. If this is about revenge against Americans or Westerners or rape and murder, we may be able to make it not worth their while," said Lily. "Robert has told us that he has an idea that might work, but he has pointed out that everything we do seems to be known to General Stratiscof. He feels that he needs to keep it secret until later."

"The plan is of no use if we are going to surrender, and it requires the help of the Russian troops as well as the Marines and all of us," I said. "I would need to talk to Lieutenant Anderson and Major Arinski to see if they would agree. Lieutenant Anderson would have to agree to fight instead of surrender, and they would both need to approve the idea. If Lieutenant Anderson won't fight, then I would need to take command or someone from our group would. I'm not sure how that could be done. It might mean we, the civilians, would have to challenge the Marines. I don't think the American Marines are going to attack American civilians, particularly women and children, even if ordered. So that shouldn't be a problem. However, we would have to show strength and will."

"That's asking a great deal from us," Jackson said. "How do we know you don't have some wild plan? After all we don't know you."

"No, you don't. Our situation is unusual and doesn't permit me time to meet each of you. As I see it the situation is fairly grim under any circumstances. I agree that surrender is out of the question, but I suspect that is what is being considered. We must act now. Does anyone else have an idea or wish to lead?"

After a silence Lily said, "If no one has any suggestion, I think we must go with Robert Jacoby, and put our lives in his and God's hands."

"Wait a minute," said the woman with the child. "Shouldn't we consider other ideas? We don't know anything about his plan. Do we really know what will happen if we give up? The president and the military must know more than we do. We should talk about this before making a decision that will affect all our lives. We could all be killed."

"What do you all say?" asked Branson. "There aren't many alternatives, and I think we all agree that we'll meet the same fate the other group met this afternoon if we surrender. No one wants that. Time is short if we're to prepare a defense, and we must act before the Russians leave. It's already beginning to get dark. Anyone else have an idea or suggestion?"

There was only the sound of people shifting their stance, and some embraced their families. The radio droned at the edge of the crowd. Finally Branson said, "I guess it's decided."

"I'll promise not to surrender and to put on the best defense possible, but I must have everyone's full support," I said. "We must stand unified or we'll all be lost. If we stand together, I believe that we'll escape and go home."

I am not sure anyone believed me.

"What do you want us to do?" asked Jackson.

# CHAPTER FIVE

Joy returned to the kitchen and looked at her to-do list. She would need to finish her grocery shopping and errands before Bobby came home from school at three o'clock. She could do the laundry while Bobby played outside, but he would want his snack first. After glancing at the television she wondered if she should try to call Robert. It was late in the afternoon there, and it was very expensive to call. However, she was worried and had not heard from him in several days. Of course he didn't call often because of the expense, and she had gotten a letter a couple of days ago. The letters were nice, but they were always a week or more old.

Considering the news she decided to try to reach

him and be sure he was all right. She picked up the cell phone on the counter and unplugged it from the charger. She found the number in the address listings and placed the call. It rang five times, and she was told that no one was available and to try again. She replaced the phone on the counter and wondered if he was busy and had forgotten his phone or if he was in trouble. She was sure that he would have notified her somehow if he had been forced to leave the clinic, unless it had been so sudden that he hadn't had time to call.

She rinsed out the coffee cups and refilled hers. She fixed a bowl of cold cereal, turned the television back on, and sat down to eat. The big story on television continued to be the rebel attack on Westerners, overshadowing the rise in oil prices and the political news, which was running at the bottom of the screen. Mark Nevin was on again along with a professor at Georgetown who was an authority on Russian affairs.

Mr. Nevin was saying that the previous slaughter was done by a small group of the rebels and not on the orders of General Stratiscof. There was no reason that he would have ordered the attack, as he had nothing to gain and much to lose in carrying it out. If that was the case, then surrender of the currently trapped group was the only logical thing to do. Mr. Nevin also pointed out that in all modern warfare both sides had killed civilians. Bombing of cities by the Germans and the Allies in World War II killed more civilians than military, and there were atrocities by both sides in most wars to the present time.

The professor acknowledged that atrocities were a part of war and were committed by both sides. He argued in this case that General Stratiscof had been reported to have been present during the attack and didn't or couldn't prevent it. If that were the case, the outlook for the present group would be grim. If the officers were not in control, there was little that could be done.

Mr. Nevin went on to say that, since the U.S. armed forces were spread so thin around the world and the Russian army was facing the main insurgent force, there were no viable military options for either country. The three hundred or so people had no chance in a fight against twenty thousand troops. Escape over the mountains was not an option either because the climb was steep and would require equipment, and the temperature was below freezing at the higher elevations. Surrender was the only choice.

The professor pointed out that the Marines and Russian soldiers were well equipped and could make a stand if they could narrow the field of attack. It would be like the Spartans at Thermopylae or the Jews at Massada. They could hold out for a while and maybe discourage the rebels, who might move on.

Mr. Nevin agreed but pointed out that in both the examples the Spartans and Jews were killed in the end.

It appeared that the pundits saw nothing but gloom and doom. Joy felt a chill. She shook it off, turned off the television, rinsed her dishes and placed them in the dishwasher. Picking up the grocery list she went for her coat and car keys. She hated to leave home as Robert might call, and she would love to talk to him. However, there wasn't anything she could do for him, and she went out to the car.

# CHAPTER SIX

I had a plan but didn't think that Lieutenant Anderson would go for it. I knew a little about him. He was young and strictly military. He was from a military family with his father having been a navy officer during the Vietnam conflict, and his older brother was a Marine lieutenant who lost both legs to a car bomb on the Baghdad airport highway and died on the way to an aid station. James graduated from the Virginia Military Institute in Lexington, Virginia, a year after his brother's death. He joined the Marines, trained at Quantico, Virginia, and, I am sure volunteered for duty in Iraq. In true military tradition he was posted to Uzbekistan, where his experience was limited to embassy duty, which was not good preparation for the present problem. However, many of the Marines in the unit had seen action in Iraq and Afghanistan, and from what I had been told his first sergeant had considerable combat experience.

I picked up the M16 that I had been given and shown how to use, and I loaded it. I told Henry Jackson to get his weapon and to come with me. Jackson was wearing a bulky sweater, long brown wool pants. and boots. I asked if he was going to be warm enough as it could be awhile before we returned. He said he thought he was fine.

I asked Lily Blackthorne and John Branson to organize the civilians. They needed to be in a defensible area with the young children and some of the women in the center. Everyone else should surround the area and keep the military out. Women and older children who could be trusted with weapons should take up defensive positions and the stronger men should be interspersed among them. I didn't think any of the Marines would attack American women and children. I told Lily to tell everybody not to shoot at anyone but to warn them off if necessary by firing in the air.

Henry Jackson and I walked toward the command post that had been set up in the tree line to hide it from the enemy across the valley. We had to climb across rocks and get through low brush in open spaces. Under the trees the ground was soft and covered with pine needles, leaves, and small stones. It was about a hundred yards between the civilian camp, which was just off the road, and the military command. As Jackson and I approached, a Marine stopped us. I told him who we were and that we wanted to speak to Lieutenant Anderson.

"Sergeant Davis, I got a couple of civilians who want to speak to the lieutenant," he called.

Sergeant Davis came out of the shadows towards

us. He was black, medium height, stocky, and wearing a camouflage uniform with a holstered pistol around his waist.

"Why do you want to see the lieutenant?" he asked.

"We and all the civilians want to know what's being planned," I told him. "Our lives are at risk here also."

He nodded and turned back toward the command area motioning for us to follow him. He led us into a small clearing with a radio sitting on a camp table. Lieutenant Anderson and Major Arinski stood on either side of the table.

Lieutenant Anderson, who was dressed like the rest of the Marines, was blond, slim, tan, and appeared like a young poster boy for Marine recruitment. Major Arinski was a little shorter and heavier than Lieutenant Anderson and had short dark hair, a red complexion and round face. He seemed to be the American idea of the typical Russian.

The lieutenant looked at Sergeant Davis and asked, "What is it, Sergeant?"

"Two civilian representatives to see you, sir," he replied.

"What do you want?" Lieutenant Anderson asked curtly.

"I am Dr. Jacoby and this is Mr. Jackson," I said. "We and the other civilians are interested in the plans for resisting the enemy. We have heard by the radio that the president has ordered us to surrender."

"That is correct," he said. "We'll send an envoy to make the arrangements in the morning. I have contacted Admiral Clark, who commands the nearest naval contingency, to have planes ready to pick us up at the airfield near here tomorrow."

"I am sorry, Lieutenant, but all the civilians have met and discussed our situation, and we don't agree with the idea of surrender. We feel that we will meet the same fate that the other group met this afternoon, and that is not satisfactory. We prefer to die fighting. Death that way will be quicker and less painful. The mothers and women are particularly concerned."

"My orders are to surrender, Doctor, and that is what will be done. The president has a better understanding of what to do than you do. There will be no debate."

"Does he really?" I replied. "We are here and some of us saw what happened this afternoon. He did not, and it is our lives on the line not his. He has to worry about the nation and what the world will think about the one remaining super power when this is over. He can blame this on Stratiscof's perfidy and condemn him, but we will still be dead. That sacrifice may work well for you and the military but does little for the mothers and their children. Can you live with that on your conscience or your record? Your brother was a hero. What will you be?"

"Leave my brother out of this. I have my orders. The military will not work if every commander does what he wants. I have to believe in the orders of my superiors."

"The president may not realize that General Stratiscof was there this afternoon when the refugees were tortured and killed. There is no way Stratiscof will let us go, and we will not surrender," I told him.

"I'm sorry, but I'm in command here and will obey my orders particularly since they come from the commander-in-chief," he replied.

"Begging your pardon, Lieutenant Anderson, but you only command the Marines and not the civilians nor the Russians. Actually Major Arinski out ranks you," I told him.

"The civilians are my responsibility and will do as they are told," he replied. "The Russians are not my responsibility and may do as they wish."

"No, Lieutenant, you do not control the camp, and we are not under your command. As you know the civilians are armed, as are the Marines and Russians. You are facing twenty thousand hostile troops with a divided camp. The Russians will leave tonight, and we will go further up the valley with them rather than face torture. You may surrender your Marines if you so desire."

"You will damn well do as you are told or I will have you disarmed and dragged to the surrender," he said hotly. He was obviously under considerable stress, and he was not as certain of his command as he had been.

"You think that the Marines will attack and shoot American women and children because you order it?" I asked. "I can see the headlines: "Marine Lieutenant Orders Attack on American Women and Children". That won't look good on the evening news and in your record, but I am sure the president will stand up for you at your trial. Are you even sure that the Marines will obey your orders? Some of the women and children are their wives and family."

"We will see about that. Sergeant, take some men and disarm the civilians and secure their camp," Lt. Anderson ordered.

"Hold on, Sergeant," I said. "The civilians are prepared to shoot anyone approaching them until I return. Lieutenant, are you ready to deal with a camp of Marines who will be divided among themselves about following orders to attack American women and children? And what will your defense be to your commander if you should live long enough to return home? I hardly think you will be given a medal for that. Give it some thought, and remember all the activities are being recorded and sent back to the U.S."

Major Arinski looked on with interest, and I asked him if his men would stay and fight if we did not surrender.

He nodded and said, "These are our enemies, and we have been fighting them for some time. Russians have a history of courage and not giving in. Remember Leningrad or Petersburg if you prefer.

"Even with the odds against us?" I asked.

"Yes," he replied. "We will not surrender. Escaping through the mountains will be very difficult even with the trained men and proper equipment. We would rather fight. We're not afraid."

"Well, Lieutenant?" I asked. "Suppose I take command. We could ask Admiral Clark to make me a temporary colonel, and that would absolve you of the responsibility of dealing with your orders to surrender and the problem you have in the camp. As for you, Major, you might not be under my command technically, but we will not surrender and will need your help. You can think about my proposal for a few minutes, but there is not much time."

"You already have my answer," Major Arinski said.

"Then it's up to you, Lieutenant. You face a divided command as the civilians are not going to surrender, and I suspect most of the Marines are against it also."

The lieutenant's lips were tight as he stared at me. "Arrest Dr. Jacoby, and then disarm the civilians as I ordered," he said.

Sergeant Davis didn't move. Finally he said, "Sir, we have no authority over the civilians and have not been ordered to surrender them. Why not contact Admiral Clark and tell him of the problem. Maybe he could suggest a solution."

"Are you disobeying my orders?"

"No, sir. I am suggesting a different approach to the problem that might save lives and keep us unified," Sergeant Davis replied.

Lieutenant Anderson thought for a moment, nodded in resignation, and said, "It would appear that I don't have much choice. Get me Admiral Clark."

Sergeant Davis went to the radio and after a minute gave the microphone to Lieutenant Anderson.

"This is Lieutenant Anderson, and I need to speak to Admiral Clark urgently," he said.

"This is Captain Harkins. What is your problem?"

Lieutenant Anderson explained what the situation was and what I had told him.

'Wait a moment," Captain Harkins said. "The admiral will need to deal with that."

It took a few minutes for the admiral to be found, and when he came on the radio, Lieutenant Anderson again explained the situation to him.

There was a long pause, and then Admiral Clark said, "You are on the scene. What do you want to do?"

'We are facing twenty thousand enemy troops, sir, and according to Dr. Jacoby the camp is divided against me. Many of the people are afraid of what will happen if we surrender. Making Dr. Jacoby a colonel would unite the camp, and I can advise him so no military errors are made. But he will not follow the president's orders to surrender; I have no choice and see no other way out of here. Also Major Arinski supports him, and the Russians will remain to fight if we don't surrender."

There was no immediate response. I recognized that the admiral might have concerns about surrendering also, but he could not countermand the president's orders.

"Tell him that by putting me in command, the decisions will be made by those whose lives are at risk. If we make the right decisions, we will survive and be heroes; and if not, we will all be dead. The latter will not be a problem for the U.S. government or the military as I will be responsible, and everyone's rear will be covered," I said. "It would appear to be a perfect solution."

Anderson relayed my message to the admiral, who then asked for my full name and address.

"I am Doctor Robert Jacoby from Maine," I said figuring he did not want more details since this was not a formal job application.

"Congratulations, Colonel Jacoby. You are now officially a full colonel in the Marine Corps for this mission. You have your orders. Keep me informed. Good luck."

Lieutenant Anderson signed off with Admiral Clark and turned to me. "You seem to have all the answers, Colonel. It must be nice to be always right."

"Nobody has all the right answers," I replied, "but no one wants his doctor or his pilot or his commander to be uncertain about what to do. Leadership is not about uncertainty. You should know that. On the other hand, as commander you should recognize your limitations and your errors and be willing to correct them. In this case we must also recognize the mistakes of our superiors and correct them. Our lives are at stake."

"All right, sir," Lieutenant Anderson said. "What are your orders?"

"Major, I need to have you organize your mountain unit to climb the steep cliff over to our left. They will start after dark and climb quietly and without lights. So they need to pick out the route they will use while there's still daylight. Also, I believe you have a radio tuned to the rebel command post. I want two men who speak the dialect to listen and pick up the way orders are given and the style in which they are given. Lieutenant, please select several men with experience in silent night fighting and have them note the movement and location of the few guards that they have. The guards will need to be removed quietly later. Sergeant Davis, please come with me."

"You can't attack twenty thousand with two hundred men," objected Major Arinski.

"We can't get out on the road," Lieutenant Anderson chimed in. "They have machine guns and mortars concentrated on the road, and they expect us to try to escape that way. It's the only way our trucks can get out, and they know that."

"I am aware of those facts," I told them. "We'll discuss it later. First I have to shut down the transmission of information to the enemy."

"What are you talking about," demanded Lieutenant Anderson.

"We have been sending General Stratiscof all our plans. How do you think that he found us up this road or even knew of our existence? As far as he knew he had all the refugees when he trapped the convoy ahead of us. There were no guards looking for other units while they were killing everyone. They took their time. And when we retreated, we were careful not to alert them. Then a couple of hours after we came down this road to hide, they came in behind us. This information had to come from us."

"We left that broken truck with vodka on it at the junction with the main road. Could that have been a clue?" asked Henry Jackson, who had been standing quietly.

"I don't think so," I said. "The truck was already there and all we did was to put some of the vodka from the plant on it. It was a good idea to give them something to drink tonight. The troops might have found the plant anyway, but a clue never hurts. They are enjoying themselves and should sleep well. We'll meet back here in thirty minutes, which should give you enough time to get your work done. I'll outline my plan for you then. Come on, Sergeant."

"Yes sir, Colonel," Lieutenant Anderson said and saluted me. Sergeant Davis and Major Arinski followed his example. I returned the salute in my best military fashion, which was probably more in the fashion of Gunga Din than the Marine Corps.

# CHAPTER SEVEN

Sergeant Davis, Henry Jackson, and I walked over to the clearing where most of the civilians were gathered. I noticed an attractive young woman with a rifle beside the crude path we were following, and an armed man among the rocks on the other side. The woman waved as we approached.

I turned to Jackson and asked him to find Lily and Branson and to have them gather all the civilians in the clearing so that I could speak to them.

As he left, Sergeant Davis commented that now that I was a colonel I could order things to be done rather than requesting. I pointed out to him that I might be a colonel, but they were civilians, and that requests and respect go further than orders with nonmilitary personnel.

While we were waiting for everyone to gather, a woman who was feeding her children hot soup from a pot heating on a camp stove offered me a bowl. I accepted and realized that I was hungry. The tomato soup tasted good. It had been awhile since I had eaten, and the next meal was in the indefinite future.

As I was eating, Roger Taylor, the CNN correspondent, came into the camp carrying a handheld camera with a long distance lens. He had excellent equipment. I remembered the graphic and detailed pictures he had taken that afternoon from a quarter mile away.

He set his camera down next to the camp stove and turned to me as I walked toward him carrying my bowl of soup.

"What have you been photographing?" I asked him after we shook hands.

"I was taking some general pictures of the army across from us for background use," he answered. "I'll send them back later this evening when I make my next report. My batteries are getting low, and I want to have enough power for tomorrow. How did the meeting with Lieutenant Anderson go?"

"Great," I said. "It was not as difficult as I'd anticipated. I think everyone realizes that they're not going to let us go. Making me a Marine colonel answers a lot of problems for them."

"I'm not sure about that. May I do an interview with the Marine Corps' newest colonel?"

Sure," I said, "but make it short as I have much to do and you need to save power."

"What did you mean that your appointment solves problems?" he asked.

"From Lieutenant Anderson's point of view it relieves him of having to deal with civilians and the Russians rebelling against his order to surrender, and he couldn't be certain that the Marines would obey his orders to attack American civilians. As for the president it answers his problem of commanding the most powerful military in the world but not having any military forces to rescue us. The same is true for the Russian government. The order to surrender was all that could be done, and that was going to be an embarrassment when we were all killed. This way I'm responsible for all that occurs as long as I don't give up. If we fail, I'll be blamed and can't protest as I'll be dead along with everyone else."

"But you have a plan," he said.

"Yes, but everyone expects that we'll be killed no matter what is done.

"After all, there are twenty thousand of them more or less and only three hundred or so of us counting the women and children. No one likes those odds," I told him.

"What's your plan, and what military experience do you have?"

"Other than two years' army duty in the States twenty years ago I have no military experience. However, what we need now is a plan for our defense in the morning, not expertise in supplies and logistics. If we can make the effort to capture us too expensive in terms of their lives, they'll move on. As for my plan for our defense I'll tell you when I explain it to everyone else. I suggest that you send what you have and shut down your equipment. Can you recharge from the truck engine?"

"A little, but the engine has to be running. No one wants to use what fuel we have to charge electrical equipment."

"Then you best send what you have and save your power for the morning."

"I have sent it along with the pictures I took earlier."

"That was fast. You're finished and off the air?"

"Yeah," Roger replied. "I will want to send the outline of your plan as soon as you have explained it."

I turned to Sergeant Davis and instructed him to take Roger's cell phone and equipment, which had been used to communicate with CNN's office.

"What are you doing?" Roger protested.

"I am preventing you from relaying our plan to General Stratiscof." I told him. "How did you think the general was learning about us? You told CNN, who told the world that we were there when the slaughter took place, showed pictures of it, told who we are, and how many of us there are, and told where we were when we retreated up this road to hide. We heard it on our radio, and General Stratiscof heard it on his radio. He understands English quite well, having spent several years in England. It would be nice if he didn't learn what we're going to do in the morning."

"Are you serious? I never meant to betray us. I didn't even think about it. After all, I'm here also and will suffer the same fate as the rest of you. I'm not a fool, and I won't send any more information without your approval. You have my word on it. "

"Apparently no one else thought about it either. You can write material on your computer but not transmit it until further notice."

Turning to Sergeant Davis I said, "Sergeant, please see that all cell phones, including military ones, are shut off and meet me back in the command area."

After Sergeant Davis left, I walked through the camp looking for Lily and John. Most of the women and children were in the clearing where the meeting had taken place. Many of the children were playing or eating, the women were cooking or fixing beds for the night, and the men were scattered through the woods carrying a variety of weapons.

Lily was with a group of women whom she was telling to fix all available food for anyone who wanted it including the men patrolling the woods. She looked up as I approached, smiled, and said, "I've heard that you're a colonel now and in command. Should I congratulate you on your promotion?"

"I'm not sure that congratulations are appropriate," I replied. "But everyone is in agreement with my command. Our people don't have to keep the soldiers at bay any longer, and everyone can come into camp to eat and be with their families. Where's John?"

"He's with some of the men forming the defense, but there have been no problems. May we hear the plans so we know what's going to happen?"

"Yes, in a few minutes. I'll tell everyone at the same time. The main reason for the secret plan is that I think General Stratiscof was learning our plans from the radio. He learned about us, what we were doing, and where we were going from the news reports that were sent to CNN. Some of what was reported may have come from cell phone conversations that were given to the news media. Sergeant Davis has taken Roger's transmitting equipment, and we are trying to stop cell phone calls. We need civilians to stop phone use as well as the military. It's essential that our plan not be revealed, as you can understand. Will you and John continue to be the leaders of the civilians?"

"Of course," she said. "I'm sure that John will agree. What do you want us to do?"

"I'll be working out the details of the plan with Lieutenant Anderson, Major Arinski, and Sergeant Davis and will ask Jackson to assist me. Then I'll return to explain it to everyone. In the meantime make sure that all the people have been fed and have taken care of their needs. Load all the essential gear on the trucks as we'll be boarding later this evening in order to be ready to move out first thing in the morning. Tell everyone to take only what is absolutely necessary."

"We'll be leaving before breakfast?" Lily asked.

"Yes, I hope so. Everyone needs to eat well this evening. No point in saving food for tomorrow."

"You don't expect our defense to take long," she said.

"We need to be prepared to move quickly when the opportunity arises."

# Chapter Eight

Joy went out and locked the door behind her. After opening the garage door, she got in the blue Chevy van, backed carefully into the street, and turned toward the mall. She thought about what she needed to do this morning. First she would pick up the cleaning and then go to the grocery store. She would return the library books on the way home, as that would only take a moment. Her thoughts turned to Robert and where he might be in light of the news report that morning. There had been nothing in the morning paper about the killing of the Westerners, but that had happened over night, U.S. time. Although Robert had not called her in several days, she had not been worried as it was often two or three days between calls. She understood that he was busy, and the nine-hour time difference was a problem. But he would have called her if he were leaving to escape the rebels. Maybe Robert was not with either of the fleeing groups.

At a stoplight she switched the radio to the news station to learn if there was any more news about the massacre, but the news was all about fashion at the opera the night before in New York City. She pulled into the parking lot for the Stop-n-Shop and found a parking spot. The cleaners were next to the grocery store, and she would go there first.

As she shifted into neutral and put on the parking brake, the radio announcer broke into the program. "This is a special bulletin from NBC News," he said. "We have just learned that a Dr. Robert Jacoby has been appointed a temporary Marine colonel and put in command of the refugee group trapped by the rebels in Uzbekistan. This is the group that reported the killing of another refugee group yesterday and was then caught by the rebel force. Admiral Clark, who is the commander of American forces in the region, made the appointment. No reason for the appointment was given, and there has been no comment from the White House. Nothing is known about Dr. Jacoby at this time. We will have further updates when more information is available."

Joy sat with her mouth open. What in the world was happening? Could this be her Robert? He was in the area, but he had no military experience. Why would he be made a colonel? She could not believe it. It must be someone else. It made no sense.

After a few minutes she turned off the engine, gathered her purse, opened the car door and got out. Still stunned she went into the cleaners, paid the bill, picked up her clothes, and took them to the car. She hung them in the car, locked it, and went to the grocery store.

Joy finished her shopping as quickly as possible and decided to skip the library. As she drove home, there was no further news about the appointment, but she was still worried and mystified.

When she turned into her driveway, she saw Janet practically floating in the air awaiting her. Joy opened the garage door with the automatic door opener and pulled into the garage. Janet, still in her bulky brown sweater and slacks, was flushed with excitement and was at the car door before Joy could turn off the engine.

"Did you hear the news?" Janet exploded. Robert has been made a Marine colonel. Nobody knows why. It's all over the news."

"Wait a second," Joy said. "We don't know that this is my husband. It could be a different Robert Jacoby. I've not heard from him, and he would have called me."

"How could it be anyone else? How many Robert Jacoby doctors could be in the area we're talking about? It has to be Robert."

"I don't know, Janet. Why would Robert be made a colonel? He has no military experience or background."

"How should I know ?" Janet replied. "Let's go inside and watch the news. We should call our friends."

"Grab some of the grocery bags as we go in, but we're not calling anyone," Joy said dejectedly. She did not need this today.

# Chapter Nine

Henry Jackson and I returned to the command area and found Major Arinski waiting for us.

"Is everything arranged?" I asked him.

"Yes," he replied. "Two of my men are monitoring the radio transmissions from Stratiscof's headquarters and they appear to be the main way he's communicating with his commanders. We have the field officers' names. Most of the orders are about setting up for tonight and nothing about tomorrow."

"That's fine," I said. The major's English was excellent, which was a good thing since my Russian left a good deal to be desired. I asked him about that while we waited for Lieutenant Anderson and Sergeant Davis.

"I learned English in school and was stationed at the embassy in Washington for several years," he told me. "A number of my soldiers speak it as well, although some of them aren't fluent. We've found it very useful to know English."

"I wish more Americans knew other languages, although, according to the British, it would be nice if we spoke English."

"It would be great if all Americans spoke at least one common language," said Jackson.

"Agreed," I replied. "By the way I understand your first name is Henry. May I call you Henry? I don't like calling you Jackson."

He laughed and said, "Yes, Henry's my name, Henry Jackson from Mississippi. Working on the oil rigs I got used to using last names. I worked the rigs for a number of years before I received the calling to preach the word."

"Were you born in Mississippi?"

"Yes, sir. I was born and raised there in a small town outside of Jackson. My father worked in a hardware store as a manager, but my two brothers worked for the oil company and got me a job when I finished high school. I was big for my age and played right tackle on the high school football team. I could do heavy work, and the pay on the rigs was good."

"Had you met John Branson before today?"

"No. I haven't worked in the oil industry for some time. Besides there are many men working on the rigs for different companies. It's not a small fraternity where everyone knows everyone else. So John and I hadn't met before."

"Did you have any sisters?" I asked.

"No. Just the three of us kids. Mom would have liked to have a girl, but it wasn't to be. Speaking of Mom I would love to have some of Mom's gumbo and some crawdaddies now."

"It sounds as if you had a nice family. How did you get into missionary work?"

"We weren't rich, but we had all we needed. I didn't feel the lack of anything. We were always a church-going family. Mom took my brothers and me to the Baptist church every Sunday morning and night as well as Wednesday night. I had a good background for mis-sionary work. I enjoyed the work on the rigs, which was hard but fun and paid well. I didn't drink so I went to church or revival meetings on shore when I couldn't get home. It was at one of the revival meetings that I was saved, and I applied to one of the Baptist Bible schools a couple of days later. When I was accepted, I quit my job, and the rest is history. After I graduated, I was asked to come here to help run the mission and to teach. I've been here for three years."

"What do you teach?"

"Everything. I teach Bible, history, math, and English to grade school kids. I'm not really qualified to teach, but I've learned the language and no one objects to my teaching. I guess that I'm as qualified as anyone here, and I enjoy the work. The kids are great and some of them have talent. I wish I could do more. I would like to come back once peace is established."

"It sounds like you've found your calling. Were you at the mission alone? I mean, were there other American missionaries with you?"

"Yes. Pastor Graystone and his wife were in charge of the mission and the school. They were from California and had been here for ten years or more. They were in the group ahead of us. They didn't want to leave but were told to by the head of our missionary office because it had become too dangerous. They were right, but we didn't leave in time. I'd been left behind to close the school and to try to hide the books, which I gave to each of the student's families. I thought that was as good a place to hide them as any. If the rebels went through the village, I'm sure they destroyed the church and school."

"You may be right, but the rebels may have missed your village."

"Wouldn't that be ironic?" Jackson said. "We run to escape the fire and end up running right into it."

As I looked around, Lieutenant Anderson walked into the small clearing followed by a corporal. Both saluted me. That surprised me, as I was not expecting it. It takes a while to become comfortable being a colonel. I returned his salute again suspecting I needed some instruction in that procedure.

"I've found six men with training in covert operations, and there may be more," he reported. "Two of them are SEALS and the others are Special Forces. They're observing the guard activities, stations, and patrol areas. The rebel troops on our side of the river are in fixed positions and are concentrating on the road. The line extends across the field and up onto the lower hill to our right. The front positions are dug in and are covering the field in front of them. Behind those is an encampment.

"In the center of the field and along the river earthworks have been set up, and behind that is what appear to be mortars. I can't make them out well but might be able to tell better from higher up. I suspect the mortars are zeroed in on the road, as they would expect us to try to escape that way.

"On the other side of the river there's not much organization. Most of the troops are scattered up the slope and into the wooded area at the top, and they appear to be drinking, cooking and lying around. There are eight soldiers patrolling at the foot of the hill, but no one is paying much attention to us. The small house part way up the hill has two guards and is probably being used as a command center."

"Very good, Lieutenant. You might want to send someone up the hill behind us for a better look while there's still enough daylight to see," I suggested.

"Corporal, find Sergeant Myerson and tell him to send a couple of men up the hill behind us to map out the troops behind the front line," Lieutenant Anderson ordered.

"Yes, sir," the corporal replied, then saluted and left on his mission.

Sergeant Davis joined us and saluted. I returned the salute in my best imitation of Lieutenant Anderson.

"Gather around," I said. "I'm going to lay out my plan. First, we're going to attack the rebels tonight."

"Sir, begging your pardon, but there's no way that forty-four Marines and two hundred Russian soldiers can attack twenty thousand rebel soldiers," Lieutenant Anderson protested.

"Relax, Lieutenant," I replied. "We don't need to attack all twenty thousand of their troops. We need only to attack enough of them to clear the road briefly for our trucks to escape. If you look at the composition of General Stratiscof's army, you'll see that there are only about five thousand trained soldiers and the rest are untrained, undisciplined, and unorganized. The majority of the troops are from two tribes, and they've been enemies for years. Look at the hill across from us, and you'll see that there's almost an avenue between the two groups. I'm surprised that they have come together at all. I suspect the common bond is robbery, rape, murder, and pillage. But that's not important. The point is that they are not unified. The general plan is to take out the guards in front after everyone is asleep; move our men quietly up the space between the tribes; capture the command center and the hilltop to our left; attack the dug-in troops from the rear; and open the road long enough for the trucks carrying the civilians to escape.

"From the command center we'll try to divert the troops holding the main road to allow our convoy to pass. If we can successfully get up to the open area between the tribesmen, we can fire into both camps. With any encouragement they'll be happy to kill each other, creating a diversion and leaving us alone. Also, by taking the command center we will cut off the leadership. That's the outline of the plan. Questions or comments?"

"Colonel," said Major Arinski. "That will require a great deal of luck. We'll have to pass between the troops without being detected, and if we are detected, we'll be very exposed. And how can we open the road and hold it open while the trucks pass when it's guarded by trained troops who outnumber us at least ten to one?"

"We will need to kill the guards quietly, which I think can be done. The guards aren't regular trained troops and aren't paying attention to us. The rest of the tribesmen are tired after a big day of rape and murder and are drinking heavily from what we've seen so far. They should sleep well. As for the other troops, they're expecting an attack from the front if they're expecting an attack at all. We'll be approaching them from the rear and with surprise should be able to push them aside enough to allow the trucks to get out. The trucks shouldn't require more than a minute or two to cross the river and be out of range. However, you're right. It will require luck and coordination to succeed."

Lieutenant Anderson asked, "If this all works and we get out on the main road, where will we go? I'm sure they'll pursue us."

"We'll go to the airport, which is about five or six miles down the road," I replied. "Admiral Clark will have his planes there to pick us up."

"We'll need to have some troops cover our escape. What will happen to them?" asked Major Arinski.

"No one will be left behind," I told them. "We'll need to mine the road and set up explosives on the field to cover our last plane's takeoff. If there are bridges along the way, we can destroy them to delay any pursuit. Do you think it can be done?"

"I don't know," said Lieutenant Anderson. "Since we brought all of our military supplies with us, there are plenty of explosives, timers and ammunition; and we have people who know how to use them. It will require everything to go perfectly, and that doesn't usually happen in battle."

"There are no other reasonable alternatives that I know of. We're faced with twenty thousand hostile troops, and given our numbers we can't defend our position for any length of time. Also, there are no better defensive positions further up the valley as far as I know."

"You're correct," said Major Arinski. "The valley has no narrow spot to defend where the difference in numbers between us would be neutralized. The river is fed by several waterfalls, which are lovely, but not escape routes."

"We'll take the steep hill with the Russian climbers, and they can help with the confusion using the mortars that are there to attack the enemy below. Major Arinski will appoint someone to command the climbers and the troops that will open an escape route for them behind enemy lines. Major Arinski, his radiomen, and Sergeant Davis will be with me to take the command center. Lieutenant Anderson will organize the commando force to eliminate the guards and will lead the force to open the road. All the trucks need to be turned around quietly to head back out. We'll find as many civilian drivers as possible since we'll need most of the military for fighting, and all military will be infantry including cooks, clerks, etcetera.

"After dark we'll put all the civilians in the vehicles, and each vehicle will need a flashlight since no headlights can be used. Finally we need a demolition crew to blow bridges, mine the road, etcetera. I'll speak to the commander of the crew. Please draw up your plans and work together to get the troops needed for each operation. The largest number of men will be needed to hit the enemy guarding the road, and a few will be required to drive several trucks. If there are no more questions, we'll meet here in two hours."

"I have a question, sir," Sergeant Davis said. "How are we going to get from the middle of their camp to the road to meet the trucks and to attack their positions across the road? We may be able to get up the hill between the tribes without detection, but we can't go through their camp without being seen. As you're aware, the troops to open the road will have to be in position before the enemy is aware in order to have any chance of success."

"Good question," I replied. "If I remember correctly from coming into the valley this afternoon, there's a fairly wide wooded defile beyond the hill across from us. It appeared to run from the top of the hill down to the road. It was rough enough that I doubt that anyone is camping in it, and it probably isn't guarded. That will be our way to the road. The attack to open the road will have to be from the road and as much behind the rebel defensive position as possible; but since the rebel camp occupies most of the valley, we probably can't get behind them completely. We'll have to be out of the valley before the enemy realizes what is happening. That may not be a good answer, but it's all that I have. I'm open to suggestions. Are there other questions or comments? If not, let's do it."

"Yes, sir."

"Yes, Colonel." Each saluted and left.

Henry Jackson asked me what was next. I sent him to gather the civilians so I could speak to them. Before that I wanted to talk to Admiral Clark.

I asked the Marine guarding the command clearing to get the admiral on the radio for me. I had no clue how to operate the radio.

After a few minutes the Marine handed me the microphone, and I was speaking to Admiral Clark. He told me that my appointment had been forwarded to the Pentagon for approval.

"Thank you, sir," I said.

"I don't know if it will be approved," he commented.

"It makes no difference either way," I replied. "By the time any action is taken, my need to be colonel will have passed. You've given us as much help as you can, and I appreciate it."

"I hope it works out well. What's on your mind?"

"I have another request, sir. There's an airport about five miles south of us. Would you send some planes to pick us up in the morning?"

"I think we can provide you some transport," he replied. "How many people do you have in total?"

"There are three hundred and fifteen including children," I told him.

"And what sort of airport are we talking about?"

"I don't know," I said. "I haven't seen it. It's probably small as I think it was used mostly for transporting vodka from the distillery. The nearby town is very small."

"Does it have a control tower or night lights?"

"It probably doesn't have a manned control tower, and I don't know about lights."

"No manned control tower is just as well for us. We'll need to use small transports. About three should be enough, but they'll have no significant fire power for fighting," the admiral said.

"I understand," I answered. "We're on our own, but I would like them to be available on very short notice starting before daylight. I plan to send a message to General Stratiscof early while most of his troops are asleep. If he holds true to what he told the president, then we'll try to be out before most of his men are aware. However, when we leave we may be pursued and would need the planes quickly."

"The planes will be nearby, and it will be arranged so that you can contact them directly," he replied.

"I appreciate your help immensely, sir."

"Have someone monitor your radio at all times, Colonel. Good luck."

We would need all the luck we could get, I thought, as I walked toward the civilian area. Most of the civilians would be less happy with my plan than the military had been. The military recognized that our situation was grave, and they would rather die fighting than surrender and be executed. But I was afraid the civilians were looking for a miracle and would object to anything less. I could understand their feelings, particularly the mothers, but I was a little short on miracles at the moment.

# Chapter Ten

Joy picked up several of the grocery bags from the back seat of her van, and Janet got the remaining ones and headed for the door. Joy bumped the van door shut with her hip and followed her.

Joy set her bags on the kitchen counter and began putting things in the refrigerator, while Janet dropped her bags next to Joy's and went immediately to turn on the television.

"Can't you wait until I have put away the groceries before watching television?" Joy asked.

"No! It's too exciting knowing someone who's on the news," Janet replied.

"I know, but let's not go crazy. I still have to put up

the food before it goes bad, and I have to get ready for Bobby to come home." Besides Joy thought if this is Robert, he's in grave danger, and I'm afraid. He's my life, and he's only your neighbor.

The commentator on television was still talking to someone about the situation in Uzbekistan and how it had begun with the Russian retaliation for rebel attacks from bases the Russians claimed were in Uzbekistan. Fighting was difficult in the rugged terrain, which limited the use of tanks and other modern equipment on the ground. The same problem had arisen in Afghanistan with the Russian invasion of that country in 1980. The United States and NATO had largely avoided the difficulty by organizing warlords in various regions to fight the war. Of course, that had left the warlords in charge after the fighting had ended.

In this event the Russians had tried to hit the terrorist camps planning to withdraw afterwards, but they had been caught in the country by rebel forces. Now the Russian army was attempting to fight its way out. They had been delayed long enough for General Stratiscof to move his twenty thousand troops up toward the Russian army. However, the general and his army were not moving rapidly because they were frequently stopping to pillage communities on the way. The present situation was a perfect example of Stratiscof's problem. His troops had murdered Westerners in the convoy trying to escape them and now had trapped a second smaller group. It was apparent that Stratiscof did not have complete control of his forces.

Joy heard all this commentary while putting away the remaining groceries. As she finished, the phone rang and she hurried to answer it hoping that it was Robert calling to say that he was all right.

"Hello," Joy said her heart pounding. She couldn't believe how nervous she was.

"Is this Mrs. Robert Jacoby?" a man asked.

"Yes," Joy replied. "Who is this?"

"I'm William Arthur from CNN," he answered. "I'm calling because I think your husband might be the Dr. Jacoby in Uzbekistan."

"My husband is there, and he's a doctor, but I don't know that he's the one on the news," Joy said.

"If he's there, he's probably the one. I presume that you have not heard from him."

"No, I have not," Joy said.

"Do you know why he would have been made a colonel in this situation? Does he have any military experience or special training?"

"No. Robert was in the army for awhile, but he wasn't an officer," Joy answered. "I really don't know anything about any appointment or what's happening there."

William asked her why her husband was in Uzbekistan and about his past history such as his age, practice, and his training. Joy told him all that she knew.

While she was talking to Mr. Arthur, the television news was interrupted for a special bulletin. Joy paused in her conversation to listen to the bulletin, which was from the White House regarding Dr. Robert Jacoby. They said that his appointment had been requested by both the Marine and Russian commanders, Lieutenant Anderson and Major Arinski. Why this request had been made was not explained. The offer of safe passage if they surrendered had been relayed to Colonel Jacoby.

No other information was currently available.

Joy returned to her phone conversation. She was asked how she felt about her husband's appointment as a Marine colonel. She didn't know how she felt. Robert was in danger, and she was not happy about that. She was terrified that he would be killed, but all she told William Arthur was that Robert was a very bright man and that he would find a way out of the present situation.

William asked her about her family, how long she had been married, the name of their child, and how old he was. Joy answered his questions, he thanked her, and the interview was over.

After Joy put the phone down, Janet asked her who had called, and she was thrilled to learn that it was a reporter.

Before Janet could ask more questions, Joy reminded her of her bridge club meeting that afternoon, and Janet left grudgingly.

Growing up in a small city outside of Boston, Massachusetts, had not prepared her for this situation, Joy thought. She had lived a sheltered existence as a child and since her marriage. The biggest events in her life had been marrying Robert and the birth of Bobby. She had no experience handling reporters and did not want to start learning now.

Joy had not been enthusiastic about Robert's plan to serve in a clinic in Uzbekistan, but she had understood his need to get away for a while after the trial. His medical group had encouraged him and even agreed to continue his salary. They seemed to think it would be good PR after the recent bad publicity, and they gave him a six months sabbatical. Of course, at that time no one knew of any particular political problems there, and it was before the Russian incursion. Even recently the fighting had not been in Robert's area of the country. How could she have known this was going to happen?

Joy decided to let the answering machine take the rest of the calls for the day. She was not in the mood to talk to more reporters or inquisitive friends.

# Chapter Eleven

The light was fading quickly and the temperature was falling as I approached the clearing where the civilians were gathered. The night was going to be cold. I looked for Henry Jackson and saw him along the edge of the clearing. He, Lily, and John Branson were standing together talking, and I joined them.

"Has everyone been fed?" I asked.

"Most of them have," Lily replied.

"Are most of them in the clearing? I would like to speak to everyone at one time."

"Yes, I think so," John said. "Let me get everyone's attention."

He walked to the middle of the clearing and called

for all the people to gather around so I could speak to them.It took a few minutes for everyone to come, and I spent the time moving to a place where everyone could hear and see me.

After they had quieted, I told them the outline of my plan. There were objections immediately from a number of people. I answered many of the same questions as had been asked before by the officers. I explained that our options were limited and that our biggest advantage was surprise. It would require coordination and luck.

A thin young girl in a large dark overcoat stood up. She looked like a child and too small to be in a strange country by herself.

"My name is Mary Marshall," she said. "I'm a Christian missionary and have been teaching at one of the schools and at the village church. One of the things I've been teaching is faith in God. Now we need to show our faith. We should all pray to God to rescue us, as there is no other way to be saved. If He will save us, we don't need to do anything else. We will be saved by our faith."

"I agree," I said. "But I would like to point out that the Lord has not sent His angels in legions to rescue anyone in several thousand years. He didn't send them to rescue Jesus from the cross. I believe He helps us by guiding people to help themselves succeed. I agree that we should pray for guidance and help to make our plans be successful. If we do nothing, our fate is sealed."

"Yes," John Branson said. "We should pray, but we should also move on with helping ourselves."

"Mary, maybe you could organize a prayer group after this meeting," I suggested. "I also need volunteers to drive the trucks. Most of the military are needed to open the road and can't be spared to drive. Please see Henry Jackson if you can drive a truck. Hold up your hand, Henry."

I turned to Lily and asked her to locate as many flashlights as she could. "We'll need at least one for each truck," I said. "When the trucks begin to move, someone will need to hold the light hidden inside the back of the truck so that the vehicle behind can see it and follow. We won't be able to use headlights, and since there will be no moon tonight, it will be dark. I could use a flashlight also."

"I'll find as many flashlights as I can," she replied. "I hope we'll have enough. If not maybe we can use candles."

"Good," I said. "The Marines are turning trucks around and lining them on the road out of view of the enemy. Later this evening would you and John get everyone on board quietly? It may be uncomfortable, but there won't be time to load once the fighting starts. And this is important. Once the trucks start there will only be a couple of minutes to get all the trucks across the stream. We cannot wait for anyone, and we cannot stop for anyone. The window of opportunity is very small. This must be emphasized to everyone. There can be no exceptions. Am I clear on that?"

"Are you speaking of literally two minutes?" John asked.

"Yes," I said. "The road will be hit by mortar shells and gunfire once they see we are trying to escape. No one will survive after that. The trucks behind will not have a chance."

They both nodded. John said, "I'll start getting everyone ready. When do you think we will need to get aboard the trucks?"

"Once they have the trucks set, you can begin loading at any time, but everyone should be ready by one a.m. You'll need to divide up the civilians to ride in the first six trucks. The soldiers who'll be picked up on the other side of the enemy camp will use the rest of the trucks. There are two hundred and sixty of them. Henry may need help with finding drivers as well."

"We'll get it done," Lily said.

As I started to leave, Mary said, "Before you go, could we sing a hymn? It might lift everyone's spirits. Then I will be glad to pray with anyone who wants me to."

"Of course," I replied.

Mary went to the center of the clearing and said, "Let's sing 'Amazing Grace'. Everyone knows that."

Slowly some of the men and many of the women gathered around her, and she began to sing in a lovely alto voice. Her voice was haunting and lonely in the quiet of the night. Gradually some of the people around her began to sing, and then more until everyone was singing. I joined them even though my voice was gravelly and off-key. It was lovely, sad, and exultant.

When we finished singing, the night was quiet except for a few distant sounds from across the valley. The crowd gradually dispersed leaving the center of the clearing with a small group around Mary.

I put on a sweater under my jacket and picked up my backpack. Also I wanted to use the latrine before heading back to the command area. I knew there would be problems and wondered what they might be. There were plenty of possibilities. I would learn soon enough, I was sure.

# Chapter Twelve

Twilight had faded into darkness. The only lights were occasional flashlights and the narrow spots of light from the fires, which were on the ground and gave only small circles of light like splotches of red with a few dark shadows sitting or moving around them. The trees rose straight and tall, and their branches blocked any view of the dark sky. There was little growth under them except for tall grass and scattered low bushes in areas where the trees had been cleared by man or nature. It was like a dark, cold cathedral.

Across the valley it was the same except there were many fires flickering under the trees and scattered in the open spaces on the valley floor and across the hillside. The enemy stretched across the valley floor and up the lower slopes of the hills. The roadway was clear and black, but the fires extended up the valley as far as I could see. It was like a mass of lightning bugs flickering along the valley.

I stopped for a moment and looked into the darkness. It was often dark at home when Joy and I went out, but it was not this black. I wondered what Joy and Bobby were doing. It would be afternoon there. Bobby would be at school, and Joy would be shopping or doing housecleaning. With Bobby there was always a great deal of picking up to be done. Joy must have heard what was going on here, but would she know that I was with this group? I wished that I had been able to contact her before I left the clinic.

It had been my harebrained idea to come here to help others in the clinic, but now it was doubtful I would see her again. I guess no good deed goes unpunished. I love her and would like to be able to put my arms around her and tell her so. I promised that if I got out alive, I would stay home, run my practice, and enjoy my family.

I put these thoughts away and began to make my way to the bottom of the hill to find our troops. Although I had a small flashlight, it was difficult to see. There were rocks and tree roots projecting all around waiting to trip the unwary. I moved slowly as there was no path to follow, and I had only a general idea of where I was going.

Although it was my plan, I knew better than to interfere in the operational details where I would be completely lost and make a disaster of preparations. However, I was the commanding officer, and I wanted to know how the planning was progressing. Besides I had nothing to do and was bored and anxious.

As I was coming out of the tree line into the tall grass, something moved out of the blackness to my right. It jumped in front of me close enough to touch me easily. I could see only the outline of a figure, but it appeared huge and menacing. I felt like a child out at night without his parents.

"Who are you and why are you coming down here? The civilian area is behind you and to the right," a male voice demanded.

"I'm Colonel Jacoby and am looking for Lieutenant Anderson and Major Arinski," I responded.

"I'm sorry, sir," he said, "but how do I know who you are?"

"You don't," I replied. "I have no uniform or identification, and you wouldn't expect me to. You need to take me to your commanding officer for identification."

"Charlie, see if you can find Sergeant Davis or Lieutenant Anderson. Tell him that the colonel is here."

"Okay, Jonsey," came the reply from the darkness, and someone moved off through the grass.

"Please turn off your flashlight, sir," Jonsey urged. "I don't think that anyone over there is paying us any attention, but there's no point in sparking their interest."

"Good point," I said and did as he requested. It was suddenly even darker. After a moment as my eyes adjusted, I could see the dark shape of the man in front of me. He had not changed his position and was still facing me with his weapon lowered.

I sat down, leaned against a tree trunk, and asked him his name.

"Sir, I am Specialist Carl Jones," he said.

"Where's your home, Jonsey? Do you mind if I call you Jonsey?" I asked. "I heard your friend call you that."

"No, sir. That's what I'm called," he replied. "My home is in Virginia near Lynchburg. It's a small town named Bedford. Have you heard of it?"

"That is in the western part of the state, isn't it? I think that there is a World War Two memorial there. Or was it World War One?"

"Yes, sir. That would be the D-Day Memorial. Nineteen men from Bedford were killed in the invasion of France. Per population that was more men killed than from any other town in the country," he said.

"Really," I replied. "I'll have to go see the memorial one day. You must have been proud growing up there."

"I don't know much about the Second World War. I did see the memorial awhile back, but I didn't understand much about it even though we studied it in school. My grandfather was killed during that war, but I don't know much about him either. My father was in the Marines in Vietnam and was gung ho military. I guess that was the reason I joined, but I hope to get a college education from the military also."

"Is there a particular subject that interests you?" I asked.

"I'd like to do something with computers," Jonsey said. "I don't know exactly what yet."

"You have plenty of time to decide. After you get to college and take a few computer courses, you'll have a better idea what aspect interests you the most. Are you into any sports?"

"I played football my junior and senior years in high

school. It was fun, but I was never really good. I couldn't make college on a football scholarship, and after Dad died we didn't have enough money for me to go."

"You must have a family at home," I said.

"Yeah. My mother and younger sister are still at home. My father died a couple of years ago. I enlisted after I graduated from high school, went to basic training, and was sent here after a year in Iraq. I thought it would be a lot safer guarding an embassy here. It looks like I was wrong about that."

"What about a girlfriend?" I asked.

"Yeah, Karen and I dated in high school. She's a year younger than I am. She went to business school when I joined the Marines and is working for a car dealer in Bedford. I miss her. We're going to get married when I get home. I guess, that is, if I get home. It doesn't look very promising right now."

"We're going to get out of here. We just need a little luck."

"A little help from God would be nice," he said.

As I looked to my left, two figures emerged from the gloom, and Jonsey turned toward them.

Charlie said, "I couldn't find Lieutenant Anderson, Jonsey, but I did locate Sergeant Davis."

I stood up and Sergeant Davis asked, "Is that you, Colonel?"

"Yes, Sergeant," I replied. "I wanted to get a feeling for how things were progressing."

"We're doing pretty well. Lieutenant Anderson is working with a group of Russian and American soldiers planning how to take out the men across the river and to open the road, that's the most difficult part of the operation. The climbers have chosen a cliff route that they think they can do in the dark and are preparing to start. The six men who'll be taking out the guards are watching their movements and planning the best way to take care of them. The radio men are still listening to the orders and conversation from the rebel command post."

"We'll need to leave a few men here to drive some of the vehicles," I ordered. "Do we know how many civilian drivers we have?"

"There are twenty-six including eleven women. Lieutenant Anderson detailed six men to drive the rest of the vehicles and to set up some explosives on our hillside to make it appear as if we're still here," he replied.

"Great idea," I said. "Since it appears that it's going well here, I'll check on the civilian preparations."

# Chapter Thirteen

I returned to the camping area to speak to Lily, John, and Henry. It was dark, but I did not turn on my flashlight until I was back in the tree line since it would be expected to be seen there. At one edge of the clearing that was being used as a meeting place a group of people were standing with their heads bowed listening to Mary speak, and I presumed that this was the prayer meeting.

I found Lily among the women and children scattered in small groups among the trees. She saw me as I walked in her direction.

"How's it going?" I asked.

"Everyone is doing as well as can be expected," she

replied. "People want to know how much of their luggage they can take with them. I have told them to take very little. I'm afraid that they aren't very happy about that."

"They may not be happy, but you are correct. There will need to be at least ten persons to each truck, and the cars and other vehicles will hold even less. It will be very tight, and the civilians will have less room than when they arrived as we won't be using all the vehicles. I suspect there'll be even less space on the planes. Everyone should take essentials only. Has everyone been fed?"

"All the children and their mothers have eaten, and there's food for the men who've been organizing the convoy. John and Henry are with them. Mary is still holding a prayer meeting, but I think most of them have eaten."

"Good," I said. "Once the trucks are in position you can load the people at any time. It would be best if the loading was done quietly and not all at once."

"John and I thought we would fill one or two trucks at a time, but everyone will be loaded by one a.m. The mothers can put their children on board when they think best. We have drivers for most of the vehicles and will have them with their vehicle then."

"Okay, and how are you doing?" I asked.

"I'm fine but tired."

"It's been a long day, and the past few days have been difficult. Why don't you sleep for awhile? Have you eaten?"

"Yes, I had something to eat earlier. If things settle down I'll catch a nap." Lily paused for a moment, and then added, "There is a problem which I hesitate to mention since we've dealt with it before."

"What's that?" I asked.

"There are several vocal people who are still questioning the course of action that we're taking. They're threatening to alert the enemy of the coming attack. We've tried to keep them under control pointing out that preparations are already underway and that this is the approach everyone has agreed upon. Even though they know that warning the enemy will mean death for us, they're alarming others who're nervous anyway."

"You think we need another meeting to discuss this issue? We have been over it before."

"It might help," Lily replied.

"Get all those who're interested in talking together, and I'll speak to them. If the enemy is alerted, we'll have a disaster."

"Maybe they just need a little reassurance," Lily said.

Don't we all, I thought, as I went down to where the trucks were being readied.

I found John Branson and Henry Jackson with the drivers and was told that all the vehicles that we would be using had been turned around and lined up to go.

"We calculate that we'll need about four or five trucks for the civilians and about twenty for the military," Jackson said to me. "That will be twelve to a truck, which will be crowded, but we want to use as few vehicles as possible. The rest will be left here. We have more than enough drivers and fuel."

"You're right that we want to use as few vehicles as possible," I agreed. "There will be a military driver for the first truck as he'll be leading and will need to coordinate with the troops. Load the people on the first trucks and bring the empty vehicles behind to pick up the military. Do we have enough flashlights for each truck to have one?"

"Yes," Jackson answered. "There are about fifty that we gathered from everyone. Each truck will have two and amazingly most of them work."

"Someone in the back of each truck, including military vehicles, will need to hold the light so that it can be seen by the following truck but not be seen from the outside. This will allow each truck to guide the one behind. There is likely to be a great deal of noise, shooting, explosions, and excitement, so those holding the lights need to be steady and to concentrate on keeping the light where the following car can see it. Trucks will have to be fairly close but use their brakes as little as possible since the brake lights can be seen."

"We could disconnect the brake lights," John suggested. "We would risk an accident, but the drivers should be able to tell if they're getting close from the flashlights."

"That might be a good idea if you think it can be done safely," I said. "You can begin loading anytime you're ready, but I would like everyone aboard by 0100 hours. We will begin our operation a couple of hours later. Since I can't predict how everything will go, I want us to be ready to move quickly."

"We'll work on the brake lights now and can begin loading whenever you want," John said. "We need to go slowly as it will be done in the dark."

"I understand, and there's one other thing," I said.

"Lily feels that we need to discuss the plan with everyone again as some are not sure this is the way they want to handle our situation. She is getting a group together now."

"We have made the decision already. What's there to discuss?" Jackson asked. "This is the only way."

"I know," I replied. "However, we must put down any dissent and give encouragement. Let's get it over with. You have a couple of soldiers to watch the trucks?"

Jackson nodded and called for the drivers to follow us up to the camp area.

We moved slowly using just three of the flashlights. When we arrived at the open area, Lily had gathered a large group around one of the fires, and we joined them.

I saw Dorothy and went to stand by her. Henry Jackson and John Branson came with me along with most of the drivers.

"What's happened so far?" I asked her.

"It's the same old stuff," she said. "That guy over there, I think his name is George or something, says we should follow the president's orders and surrender. He doesn't believe that this plan will work and we can't fight our way out. A couple of people agree with him. A few people think George is crazy and that we'll all be slaughtered like the other group today. Most people are afraid and don't know what to do."

"What do you think?"

"I believe you're right that we have no choice except to try to fight our way out. I only met you this afternoon, but I trust you," she replied.

"Thanks," I said. "I need all the support I can get

since no one here knows me very well."

Lily saw me and said, "Let's hear what Colonel Jacoby has to say. It's his plan, and he's the one we all supported this afternoon."

George, or whatever his name was, sat down on the ground, and I stepped a little closer to the fire.

"Since I don't know what's been said up to this point, and we have discussed the situation at length before, let me ask a couple of questions," I began. "I presume that we all agree that the twenty thousand or so forces opposite us are hostile and that they're the ones that brutally killed the group of refugees we were planning to join. Does anyone believe that General Stratiscof was not present when the killings took place? If so Roger Taylor can show you pictures of him there with his officers."

No one said anything and after a moment I continued. "Although it's not in his best interest to harm foreigners, it's evident that he's unable or unwilling to control his men. I suspect it's the former and that he's not going to send some of his troops against the majority to prevent a similar outcome tomorrow. He needs all his forces for the coming battle and, if the rebels win, he needs to maintain control of all the rebel force afterwards. Therefore, surrendering to him will produce the result we saw earlier today and can't be an option. It's also apparent we can expect no aid from any other source. If the U.S. president could have sent aid, he would have protected the group in front of us. We're on our own."

I paused and looked around at what I could see of the group. There were about thirty people present and they seemed to be listening. Many of the families weren't there as they had children to care for.

I continued. "We don't need to fight all twenty thousand of their men. We only need to create a hole through their lines for a few minutes to allow us to escape. We'll have the element of surprise and should be gone by the time they've recovered."

I paused again. "It's not a slam dunk, but I think we have a good chance to escape. When we get out, navy planes will pick us up at the airport."

I looked at Lily and then at Dorothy and said, "We will need God's help to make this work and should pray for that. Are there any questions or comments? We must be unified as there are plenty of enemies out there. We don't need any in here."

George stood and said, "I think that the president has more information than we do. He has the advice of the military leaders at the Pentagon and he has information from the CIA. We have none of this. We should trust his judgment. If he's right, we don't need this risky plan."

"Actually, in this case we have more information than the president since we saw the events this afternoon," I replied. "He also has more considerations than we do. He has to be concerned about the whole country while we need only be concerned about our survival. In all honesty, I don't believe he had any alternative except to recommend our surrender. The American military is stretched to its limits, and putting in a small force would not help as it would be defeated. There aren't enough forces in our region to take on this size army, and if there were a force available, it couldn't get here in time to rescue us. Therefore, the president accepted General Stratiscoff's assurances as the only choice."

"You don't believe the president would sacrifice us, do you?" George asked. "That would be crazy."

"He wouldn't if he could avoid it, but I don't think he can avoid it. According to the radio many people see no other alternative. We have another choice, and we must use it, particularly since General Stratiscof thinks we must surrender."

There was a silence while everyone thought about my points.

Finally George said, "All right. I may not agree completely, but you're probably right, and there's little time for debate. We must decide now. I support your plan. What is next?"

"Are there any other questions or comments?" I asked. I looked around at the gathering. There was some rustling. But no one spoke. George must have been the leader of the resistance, and with his support there seemed to be agreement on my plan.

"If there are no other comments or questions, we can begin loading the trucks. It must be done quietly. There's no rush, and you'll be on the trucks for awhile. Lily Blackthorne, Henry Jackson, and John Branson will give you directions. Let me emphasize that it must be done quietly and in the dark. When the trucks depart, it will be suddenly. They'll wait for no one nor stop for anyone. We'll have only moments to cross the river and pass through their camp. I can't stress this too much. The trucks can't stop nor wait for anyone. If one of the trucks stops, it will risk the lives of all those who're behind them as well as those on board. Please be on the trucks and have your families on as well. I believe this plan will work and we'll be safe."

Lily stepped forward and offered to help anyone needing her. I went to meet Lieutenant Anderson and Major Arinski. The decision had been made again, and I was responsible.

As I turned to leave, Dorothy took my arm and asked to talk to me for a few moments. She led me to a cleared area where she had her open bed roll and backpack set at the base of a large spruce tree, whose lower limbs were forty feet up. It was dark as the tree limbs intermingled above our heads blocking all view of the sky so that what little light there was from the stars didn't reach the ground.

"Do you really think we're going to get out of here?" she asked. "I know what you told everyone back there, but is that really the case as you see it? I saw what happened this afternoon, and we're facing the same men."

"As I said, I think we have our best chance following this plan. We all know the odds, but I think, if it goes as planned, we'll escape and get to the airport where the navy planes will pick us up," I replied. "I know you're concerned, but why are you asking me in private?"

"I saw what happened to Ann, who was at the mission with me," Dorothy said as tears ran quietly down her cheeks. "When I looked around at what was going on, I couldn't believe it. She was a good person, but they raped her. Gangs of men. They used her body and mouth repeatedly. I couldn't watch. It was the same for the minister and his wife, and she was old. If that's what is going to happen to me and us, I would rather die now. I've been through it before. I couldn't stand it."

She was crying harder now. I put my arm around her to comfort her. With my other hand I took out my handkerchief and pressed it to her face. She took it and stood back.

"I'm sorry," she said. "I didn't mean to come apart like that. I just had to tell someone. Everyone is busy and under the same stress. I'm sorry."

"Do you want to talk about it?"

"Do you have time?" she asked.

"There isn't much for me to do now," I said. "I laid out the general plan, and people with a lot more experience are putting it into motion. There's not much for me to do except to stay out of the way, solve problems if they arise, and push the start button when it's time to go. Why don't you talk to me? I can be a good listener."

"All right," she said. "I would like that."

She sat down on her open bed role and wiped her face.

"When I was a little girl, we lived next to the church in a small white house with blue trim and a porch on the front. There were two large oak trees in the front yard, and the backyard was open with flower beds next to the house. Mom planted herbs and mint as well as flowers. She loved roses, and there were climbing roses on the split rail fences at the end of the yard as well as several bushes in the flower beds. When the roses bloomed they were beautiful, white and red, and attracted bees from all over. They smelled nice, but you had to watch out for the bees. There was a grape arbor next to the garage on the right of the yard. It produced sweet grapes, but it attracted the bees as well. The center of the yard was open so my brothers and I could play, and there was a small sandbox just outside of the kitchen door. Mom could watch us from the kitchen window.

"Our house had two stories, and my bedroom was on the second story in front looking out over the street. There was a streetlight out front, and it shone in my window making shadows on the ceiling. I loved my room and always felt safe there. It had a small dressing table and a closet with a full length mirror on the door. I had a single bed with rounded wooden bed posts and a three-drawer bureau. My parents painted the room light pink with white trim at my request. I could read at my dressing table or on my bed. Sometimes at night I would read by the street light after I was supposed to be asleep. I loved to read and would pretend that I was the heroine in the story I was reading.

"The town was small, and we knew most of the people. My two younger brothers and I had to be the perfect children. We were expected to do well in school, which wasn't a problem as I liked school. Despite having to be in church on Wednesday night, twice on Sunday, and attending other events, I liked church also. When I was eight, I began singing in the choir and enjoyed that. We practiced before church on Sunday morning and Wednesday evening. Though I wasn't an outstanding singer, I was allowed to sing a solo on occasion. Our lives revolved around church and school. Even in the summer my brothers and I went to a church camp. I had a few friends, but none were close. I guess that was because I was the preacher's daughter. I played with my brothers who were two and three years younger than I was, and we got along well. We weren't rich, but we had a nice quiet life.

"I particularly remember Christmases. Although we didn't have the snow of the typical New England Christmas, it was a warm and loving time of the year. All the store windows had lights and trimming, and the air was filled with song and anticipation. We decorated the church with candles in the windows, wreaths on either side of the choir, and a small tree on one side decorated with lights, crosses and paper angels made by the younger children. On the end of each pew we hung evergreen branches, which made the church smell like pine trees. We sang Christmas carols, and on Christmas Eve everyone held a lighted candle and sang "Silent Night" with the lights out. It was so beautiful, and I loved it.

"At home we had a wreath on the front door and trimmed a tree in the living room with strings of lights, old glass balls, strings of popcorn, and tinsel. There were lots of packages under the tree, and I loved wrapping the few gifts I could afford for my family. People from the church dropped by to visit and left food and presents. Christmas day, before we went to church to hear my father preach, we were allowed to open our stocking presents, which were usually oranges and nuts, socks, and toothbrushes, and things like that. After the church service we had a big dinner, and then all the presents under the tree were opened. It was a wonderful and loving time for me.

"But when I was twelve, things changed. I developed breasts. Even though we weren't allowed to wear revealing or stylish clothes, I was teased by both the girls and the boys at school. I hated going to gym because the girls made nasty comments about my breasts, and in the halls some of the boys would snap my bra. I complained to the teachers, but they told me it was just a stage and it would pass. Nothing was done, and I began to dread going to school. My grades suffered also. And then at night my father began coming into my room."

I turned to look at Dorothy. She was looking down at her hands, and I knew what was coming. She looked up at me with tears running down her cheeks and said "I have never told anyone about this except my mother. But I want to get it off my mind before…whatever."

"I understand," I told her.

"Anyway," she continued softly, "at first he just sat on my bed and talked to me. And then on later visits he began to rub my back and then my breasts. I was humiliated. My body became rigid, and I tried to blank out what was happening. After a few minutes he would leave, and I would cry myself to sleep.

"I tried going to bed early and pretending to be asleep. Sometimes he would leave me alone, but often he came in anyway. I told my mother, who said not to tell anyone, but she never did anything about it. I felt as if no one would help me. It got progressively worse, and I thought I would have a mental collapse. Then one day my mother came into my room and told me I was going to live with my grandparents in South Carolina. My mother drove me to my grandparents' home and left me. Shortly thereafter my family moved to another town in Texas to a new church, and I didn't see them for a long time. I don't really know what happened. My grandparents were good to me, and I stayed with them until they both died a couple of years ago. After they died and I graduated from Bob Jones University, I joined a missionary group and came here."

"You know that none of what happened was your fault. You were just a child and did nothing wrong," I told her.

Dorothy looked up at me again and said, "I understand, but you don't feel worthy if your own parents don't care about your. I know that it doesn't make sense, but that's the way I feel."

"You're very worthy. Coming here to teach children was not easy. That took a lot of courage and would not have been done by someone who didn't care about people. You should be proud of yourself and move on with the rest of your life. Decide what your want to do with your life: marriage, children, or a career. Consider going back to see your brothers and parents so that you can put all this behind you. I would guess that your brothers would love to see you and learn about your adventures here."

"Do you think so?" she asked.

"I'm sure of it," I said. "They love you and wonder what's happened to you. I doubt that your parents told them the truth. Don't be too hard on your mother. She probably arranged for you to go to your grandparents to protect you."

She stood and hugged me. "Thank you. You are probably right about Mom. I didn't think about that. When we get back home, I will go see my family. Thank you."

# Chapter Fourteen

As Joy listened to the CNN news report, they gave all the information that she had given to William Arthur. Beyond that there was nothing new.

There had been numerous phone calls including many from news agencies and a few from friends. All the reporters had the same questions. What were Robert's qualifications for command? How did she feel about his appointment? Why had he been appointed commander? Mostly these were questions to which she had no answer.

Most of the calls from friends were congratulations, and only a few recognized her anxiety and the danger that Robert was in. These latter offered any help they could give. Joy let the answering machine take most of the calls.

She fixed a sandwich for lunch, which she ate hurriedly, prepared half a peanut butter and jelly sandwich for Bobby, and folded a load of clothes. She expected Janet and her bridge club to come over to discuss all the morning's events, but they didn't. She was grateful for that. She hoped that Bobby would play with Carl Leveret, a neighbor's son, and give her more free time.

Bobby came rushing excitedly in the back door, dropped his backpack on the floor, and ran to his chair. It was obvious that he had heard the news, and he would be pleased that his dad was a Marine colonel. After all, that didn't happen every day.

Joy poured a small glass of milk for Bobby and put it in front of him.

"Mrs. Leveret said that Dad has been made a colonel in the Marines. Is that true?" Bobby asked as soon as he sat down.

Joy looked at her son for a moment realizing that everyone was aware of Robert's situation, and then she sat in the chair next to him. She wondered how much she should tell him. Finally she said, "That appears to be true, but he's in danger too."

"Why? What's happening? Mrs. Leveret didn't tell me much except to go home. I wanted to play with Carl this afternoon and was going to call you to ask if that was all right," Bobby said.

Joy explained what she knew, but left out most of the unpleasant things. Bobby stopped eating. He looked up at her and tears rolled down his cheeks. She knew that he had picked up on her fears.

"Dad will be all right, won't he?"

She leaned over to him and put her arms around him. "Of course he will. We'll pray for him," she said, with more confidence than she felt.

She wiped the tears away with his napkin and realized that everything in life had changed since this morning. Both their little worlds were upside-down.

Bobby recovered quickly and accepted her explanation. He stopped crying and went back to eating his snack. Joy slumped in her chair and was glad that Bobby was better, but she wondered how she would cope if something happened to Robert. She couldn't imagine life without him.

# Chapter Fifteen

After leaving Dorothy, I returned to the command area. Lily and Henry were organizing the civilians, and I was confident that they would be ready in the next few hours. Most of their time would be spent waiting and quieting the anxiety that everyone felt. That would be their main problem. If all went as planned, the whole operation should take less than an hour. The time frame to get the trucks through the enemy lines and to the airport had to be brief because surprise was our major weapon, and it would not last long.

At the command post I found Lieutenant Anderson sitting on an old tree stump and Jonsey at the radio, which was on a field table with an oil lamp beside it.

The lamp provided bright light compared to the surrounding darkness. The trees appeared as black ghosts against the clear sky with bright stars scattered across it. There was no light pollution here except for the tiny man-made flickering fires on both sides of the valley, and these were lost in the vast darkness.

Anderson rose as I approached and saluted. He was wearing a field jacket as was Jonsey. The temperature had dropped considerably since sunset. I returned the salute and asked how the preparations were going.

"I wanted to present my plan for your approval," Lieutenant Anderson said.

I nodded and said, "Let's get everyone together since all the plans must be coordinated." I really wanted the opinions of people with military experience since I had essentially none.

Lieutenant Anderson sent a Marine to get Major Arinski, his aide, and Sergeant Davis.

"Have there been any further communications from the navy?" I asked.

"No, sir," Jonsey replied.

"Where did you get the oil lamp?"

"It was in one of the vehicles," Jonsey said. "I think they came from one of the churches. We requisitioned it. I don't think the missionaries were happy, but I thought we had priority."

"Of course," I replied. "It won't make any difference in the long run as the lamp can't go with us anyway."

Just then Major Arinski with several Russians, along with Sergeant Davis, and an army corporal appeared like apparitions out of the night. Everyone gathered around the table.

"Let's run the operation from the beginning with Major Arinski," I said. "Are the climbers set? How are the radio men coming?"

"I have two men who speak the dialect listening to their radio transmissions, noting the orders given, and to whom they're given. They think they can imitate the commands so there won't be any questions," Arinski said. "We know the commanders in each area by name and their radio operators. The nine climbers have begun their ascent and will rest in a spot just below the top. It's not a long climb, and it should be easy even in the dark. Once the shooting starts below them, they'll attack. Although they're a small number, there should be no problem killing everyone. Once the area is secured they'll use two or more of the mortars to fire into the camp below and on the other side of the river. They'll avoid the road and hit the area well away from our forces. Once our troops come up the other side, they'll all leave immediately and join us on the road beyond the camp."

"Good," I said. "Are there any comments or questions?"

Lieutenant Anderson looked up from the table and asked how many radios we had.

Sergeant Davis said there were four. One had been given to the climbers, one to Lieutenant Anderson, one to the engineers, and one to the command group. All the others had been used for parts.

"There are none for the civilians?" I asked.

"No," he replied. "When the road is cleared, Lieutenant Anderson will have to send someone to start the trucks across the river."

"That will take too long," I said. "Sergeant Davis, co-ordinate with Lily Blackthorne or Henry Jackson. Have a couple of civilians hidden along the side of the road, spaced out enough that they can communicate with flashlights. They can relay the signal back to the first truck and be picked up as the trucks go past. What about the guards?"

"Yes, sir," he replied. "As for the guards, there are only about six of them, and they're standing in groups of two talking. Taking them out will not be a problem. Once that's done, our men will signal us and lead the way up between the camps. We'll need to move across the field quietly and quickly and hope that no one sees us."

Lieutenant Anderson told me he would have about one hundred and sixty troops to clear the road; fifteen would stay at the top of the hill and help where needed; ten would move behind the camp to get the climbers back to the road; forty including the engineers would commandeer vehicles and clear the road beyond the camp to the main road; and five would go with Major Arinski, Sergeant Davis, and myself to take the head-quarters. Everyone else was either a driver or doing some specific project.

"The engineers will destroy the other enemy vehicles that we don't need," Lieutenant Anderson said, "They'll plant explosives on the roads and bridges to slow down any pursuit after we've cleared the area. They'll also need to place devices to protect the last plane as it leaves. That will leave less than ninety men to open the road for the civilians and trucks."

He went on to explain that he had divided his troops

into three groups with Russians and Americans in each group who could speak to each other. Many more Russians spoke English than Americans who spoke Russian. One group would attack along the edge of the road and clear enough space for the trucks carrying the civilians to pass; the second and third groups would hit the area from behind, with the second group taking out the mortars and the third group providing covering fire for the escape. They would all be evacuated in the vehicles at the end of the convoy from our camp. There were plenty of vehicles, but we needed civilian drivers at least to get the vehicles across the river.

"I believe there will be enough drivers to meet the need. All of you have done a good job. Let's make it work. Are there any other comments?" I asked.

No one said anything.

"Then I guess we're set. We'll start our operation at 0230 hours to 0300 hours. Sunrise is about 0600 hours, but we may have to fly out before then. If the airport doesn't have lights, which is a good possibility, we'll need to park vehicles along the runway to provide enough light for the planes to land and take off. Since we must attack the rebels while they are asleep and they tend to arise early, I'm afraid to wait past 0300 hours. If all goes well, we'll meet on the road to the airport or at the airport in an hour after we start. I hope that there will be at least one major river bridge that we can destroy and that there'll be enough confusion that there won't be any organized pursuit. However, I think we have to be prepared to evacuate in the dark.

"One more thing," I added. "I want to bring out our wounded and dead where possible. I don't want to put additional lives at risk, but where possible I would like to bring out the dead and wounded. If there's no further business, Sergeant Davis and I will check on the civilians while you complete your preparations. We'll meet back here at 0130 hours."

# Chapter Sixteen

Bobby seemed fine after Joy spoke to him; after finishing his sandwich and milk, he went out to play. Kids were resilient. Nothing seemed to bother them for long.

Joy had just cleared the table from Bobby's snack and sent him out to play with Carl when Janet knocked on her kitchen door. Janet had changed into a dark gray dress, gray pumps, and a brown wool jacket. She had also put on lipstick and eye makeup. Joy opened the door and let her into the kitchen.

"I don't have any coffee made," Joy said. "How about a Coke?"

"That would be fine. I had plenty of coffee at the book

club," she replied. "Have you heard any more news? Robert's appointment was the main topic of conversation at the book club. We hardly mentioned the book in all the excitement."

"I'm sure," said Joy going to the refrigerator, pouring two soft drinks into glasses, and bringing them to the kitchen table where Janet was sitting. "I haven't watched the news since this morning, but I don't expect anything new since it's night over there now."

"Well, we watched several news broadcasts during the meeting, and you're right that there isn't anything new from there. However, in view of the terrible massacre of foreigners yesterday everyone is demanding that the president do something to save Robert and his group. It's the main story on the news."

"Is the president going to do anything to rescue them?" Joy asked.

"So far the White House has only said that they had a promise from the general in command of the insurgent troops that he would guarantee their safety if they surrendered in the morning. A few commentators think that they would be fine if they were left alone, but most feel that the fact that he's brought his entire army in pursuit of them is a bad sign. The president seems to believe the general's promise. I don't think he plans to help them." Janet finished part of her drink and set the glass on the table.

Joy looked down at her hands folded on the table and felt like crying for the first time since this whole episode had begun, but she would not let Janet see her cry. "Maybe something is being done, but they don't want to tell everyone about it," Joy said. "If we were planning an attack, we wouldn't want to announce it to the world."

"I'm so sorry. I'm stupid," Janet said. "You're worried about Robert, and I'm going on about how bad everything is. I was excited and didn't think about how you would feel. You're right. The president would not announce a rescue to the world. That would be dumb."

Janet came around the table and put her arms around Joy's shoulders. "Why don't you and Bobby come over for dinner this evening?" she asked.

"Thank you, but I'm fine. I already have a chicken roasting in the oven, but I do appreciate the offer."

"All right, but if there's anything I can do, please let me know," Janet said as she hugged her.

Joy closed the door behind Janet and sat back down at the table. She looked at her wedding ring and thought that she had loved Robert from the moment she had seen him. They had met in Boston at the Oyster House one beautiful fall day when she and two friends went in for lunch. Robert had been there with a friend who knew Emily, one of Joy's companions. Robert was medium height with short curly brown hair and a winning smile. Joy remembered that he was wearing dark brown pants with a light turtleneck sweater under a tweed jacket. She had thought him very attractive.

After a year of dating they had married and lived in Boston for two years while Robert completed his schooling, and then they had moved to Bangor, Maine, where he had taken his internship and residency in internal medicine. After his three-year residency Robert had elected to join a group of internists in Bangor, and he had been made a partner after another five years.

He was doing well until that day two years ago. Joy had never understood the details of what happened, but Robert and his group had been sued for malpractice. It had something to do with a missed or wrong diagnosis in a young pregnant woman with severe high blood pressure. The baby had died. A year later Robert had been cleared, but he had continued to feel guilty and depressed. Although his partners and friends had pointed out that he was not at fault, he blamed himself and decided to take six months off to work at the clinic in Uzbekistan.

Robert was a good father and husband. They had not had any serious fights, although she had not been happy when he decided to take these six months at the clinic. But she had never thought that she would lose him. Well, someday when they were old, maybe, but not now. She couldn't even conceive of it.

Tears slowly ran down her face, and she prayed for Robert's safe return. They attended church regularly, and she believed in God. After all she had been blessed with a wonderful marriage and family. God would not desert her now. He would bring Robert home.

She wiped the tears from her face with a tissue and went to check the chicken in the oven. Life went on, and she had to keep it as normal as possible for Bobby.

# Chapter Seventeen

Sergeant Davis accompanied me under the tall trees, across the path leading to the open field and the river, and around the curve of the hill to where the road ran at the hill's base. There were fewer fires on the hillside across from us now, and they appeared as penlights against the dark hillside. Although it appeared that the enemy was retiring for the night, we kept our flashlights pointed toward the ground to avoid being noticed just the same.

The first of the trucks was dark, but there was activity around the third and fourth trucks. When we reached the rear of the third truck, we found Lily Blackthorne and Henry Jackson talking to a woman and her son, who was sitting on the tailgate of the truck.

"You need to use the latrine now. We don't know when we'll have the opportunity later," Henry said to the boy reasonably.

"It's cold, and I don't need to go," the boy replied.

"Put your coat on, Jake, and go with Henry and try," his mother said. "Then you can come back and go to sleep. I have a blanket for you so you'll be warm."

Grudgingly Jake slid off the truck and went with Henry.

"Jake isn't usually so uncooperative, but he's upset and tends to be combative when he's afraid," his mother said. "I'm Susan Alvoid and worked at the legation. Jake's father was in the army and was killed in Iraq two years ago. Jake misses him. Now there's just Jake and me. I took this job to support us, although I didn't want to work overseas. But you have to take what's available." She hesitated a moment and then added "I'm sorry. You can't be interested in my story when you have bigger problems. It's just that I get so lonely and afraid sometimes as Jake is the only family I have. I'm fine. I'll get Jake in the truck when he gets back."

Susan was a pretty young woman with long blond hair under a white wool cap. She had a round face that was flushed in the cold, and her speech had a western twang. She wore a hip-length dark jacket that appeared to be stuffed with down and an ankle-length skirt over black boots.

"We understand, Susan," I told her. "We're all tired and anxious after a very difficult day. I'm Dr. Robert Jacoby, and if I can do anything for you, please let me know."

"I've seen you, Dr. Jacoby, and appreciate all that

you're trying to do for us. We won't be a problem."

"You're not a problem, Susan," Lily said. "Everything will be fine. Henry and Jake should be back in a minute. Why don't you get in the truck, and Henry will get Jake in."

"Thank you," Susan replied. Sergeant Davis helped her into the truck where she sat on the end of the bench. The remainder of the truck was full.

"Do you have family back in the States?" I asked Susan.

"I have a sister in Kansas. She's married and has two children of her own, a boy and a girl, but I haven't seen them in more than a year since Jake and I were assigned here. Both my parents died several years ago. My husband, Alex, was in the Army National Guard, and his unit was activated to serve in Iraq. He was in the military police, and I guess they needed them. Both his parents died when he was young, and he was raised by an uncle. So it is pretty much Jake and me."

"If you need any help when we get back, my offer applies there as well," I said.

"Thank you" Susan said, "but I'm sure the government will have another job for me. They take good care of us."

"I'm sure they do," Lily said.

Henry and Jake returned, and Henry lifted Jake onto the truck where he sat on the floor in front of his mother. "He should be all set now," Henry told her. "See you later, Jake, and you take care of your mom."

Henry turned to Lily and told her that there was a problem with the people in the truck behind us.

"What sort of problem?" Lily asked.

"You don't want to know," he said with a smile. "You would think when faced with this sort of situation, people would not be so petty, but I'll take care of it."

"Thanks," I said to his back as he walked off.

I looked at Lily, who was still wearing her long coat and appeared warmer than I felt.

"Most of the people are already in the trucks," she said. "Each truck has someone to hold the flashlight. They'll sit up in the truck so that only the truck behind can see the light. We have Marine drivers for the first and last truck, and civilians will drive the rest."

"Great," I replied. "Everyone should be ready to leave instantaneously from around two o'clock on. It will probably be later than that when we actually go, but I want everyone to be ready."

Sergeant Davis then informed Lily that he needed four or five civilian volunteers to form a communications link along the road when the military advanced. He told her the purpose and asked her if she and Henry would ask for the volunteers. She told him she and Henry would take care of it. Sergeant Davis said that he would be back to pick up the people in about an hour and disappeared into the night.

Lily walked to the front of the truck and leaned against the fender. I went with her and asked how she was holding out.

"I'm fine," she said. "I'm just tired like everyone else. How are you doing?"

"Like most of the troops I'm running on adrenalin, I guess. I don't feel tired, and I should considering that we've had such a long and harrowing day."

"I'm surprised that you don't feel any pressure. You've

taken on a tremendous responsibility," she said.

"Not really," I replied. "I laid out the general plan and let everyone do their thing. If all goes well, I get to be a big hero even though I haven't done much. If it all falls apart and is a disaster, I'll regret it for the rest of my life, which won't be that long. This is the only way that I see out of here, and I feel I've done my best. Really I don't feel much pressure, but I do feel anxious about the outcome of the operation."

"Well, I've supported you, and I feel pressure and responsibility," Lily replied. "I need a cigarette."

She dug into her coat pocket and found a crushed pack. Shaking out the next to last cigarette she put it between her lips and lit it with her lighter.

"Those will kill you," I told her.

"Not in time," she laughed. "Do you really think this will work, and we won't be killed?"

"Actually, I think we have a good chance of success. No one thinks we can escape or that we have a chance of a successful attack. That's the reason that I think it might work. At worst we'll all die quickly and less brutally than the group today. At best most of us will get out."

"I hope you're right," she said taking a long drag on her cigarette.

"Tell me a little about yourself. Coming out here doesn't suggest that you're the pessimistic type."

She propped herself up on the fender and flicked the ashes off her cigarette.

"What would you like to know?" she asked.

"Whatever you'd like to tell me."

"Well, I was born in Milton, Delaware, sixty-one years

ago, and was Lily Wilson," she began. "We were a few miles from the coast and could go to the beach easily whenever we wanted. In the summer Mother often took us to Rehoboth Beach for the day. Dad was always working. It was about forty minutes away, and I remember playing in the sand and splashing in the water while Mother sat under our umbrella. She packed us sandwiches for lunch and fixed dinner at home in the evening. When I was older, we spent more time at the beach. I remember the white sand with the waves breaking gently on the shore. The boardwalk was behind the beach in town and had stores and restaurants. In the evening after changing clothes we ate at the Avenue Restaurant or sometimes the Dinner Bell, and then we would walk on the boardwalk or play miniature golf. At night you could look out over the dark water and see ship lights and sometimes the lights from the beach at Cape May, New Jersey, across the entrance to the Delaware Bay. I thought it was beautiful even when I was a child.

"Winters were usually mild in Milton, but occasionally we had snow. We lived in a big old house in the center of town and were fairly well off as my father owned the grocery store. When my brother and I weren't in school or at the beach we fished or played in the Broadkill River, which runs through the center of town. Milton is a small town, and it was fun growing up there. However, as I got older, I thought it was boring and wanted to go where there was more excitement. At the same time I was required to spend most of my free time helping my father in the store, which was actually good experience although I didn't think so at the time. Initially I helped stock shelves and later learned the cash register and to keep the account books and place orders.

"I went to college at the University of Delaware in Newark and majored in history. I had planned to teach high school, but I met Howard Blackthorne. He was a law clerk in town, and we met at the library while I was studying and he was doing research. He was several years older than I but was bright and charismatic. I mean that in a good way. We married a couple of years later, and I never taught school after graduation. We settled in Silver Springs, Maryland, and Howard joined a large law firm in Washington.

"We had three children, two boys and a girl, and I raised the children while he worked. When the children were young, I took them to Rehoboth Beach for the summer, and Howard came down for the weekends. We bought a house in the first block of Oak Avenue. It was a nice cottage with a few bushes out front and pine trees in back. The walk to the beach was less than half a block and it was only two blocks to the boardwalk. There wasn't much traffic in the area, and I felt that the children were safe. You can tell I loved it there. Anyway, my children had the same experiences that I had growing up at the beach, and that was good.

"I should mention that I became active in the peace movement after my younger brother, Billy, was killed in Vietnam in 1970. He was single. I helped organize several rallies, but my main interest remained my children. Besides, Howard didn't approve of my antiwar activities, although he understood how I felt.

"Howard died eight years ago of pancreatic cancer, and the children are grown, married, moved away and have children of their own. I have seven grandchildren.

"I felt that I needed to do something besides visit the grandchildren, so I went back to school to update my teaching skills. I've always been somewhat of an organizer since working at my dad's store, and I worked for a couple of years at the office of The World Children's Education Fund while I took night courses in education. A year or so ago I was asked to teach at a school here, and I took the job. It allows me to teach during the fall, winter and spring and to visit my family during the summer. Now I'm not only teaching but am the principal at the school. As with many of the people with us I was advised to leave when the rebellion began. I missed the first group that left, since I was trying to set up classes for the teachers who live here and would keep the school open."

"It sounds as though you've had an interesting and full life," I said.

"It has been good," she replied, "but this is a little more excitement than I like. I like to be in control. It makes me feel comfortable."

"I don't think anyone would disagree with you. I'm in charge but not in control of the situation," I said.

Lily flicked her second cigarette away after crushing it out. "Maybe I'll give up smoking if I get out of here alive."

"That would show that you were in control," I said.

# Chapter Eighteen

After leaving Lily to get the civilians settled in the trucks and to prepare them for the night's activities, I walked back through the civilian camp. Abandoned suitcases and personal items were scattered everywhere. All the important things that had been brought when the escape from violence began now had to be left in an effort to save our lives. Embers from several fires glowed in the darkness, and there were a few people still wandering through the area. Some people were sitting or kneeling on the ground sorting through their possessions trying to decide what they could take with them and what they must leave.

Squatting next to one of the fires was Mary, the

young woman who had organized the prayer meeting. She had a sheath of papers in her hand and was sorting through them. I stopped next to her and watched as she looked at each paper.

"Hello, Mary. What are you doing?" I asked quietly trying not to startle her.

She looked up at me for a moment and then said, "I'm looking at some of the pictures that the children in my Sunday school classes drew for me. I hate to leave them behind, but I haven't room to carry them. I can probably take one or two folded in my pocket, but I can't decide which to save. They're all wonderful and were selected out of the large number I had initially."

"What are they pictures of?"

"Everything," she answered. "There are pictures of their village, animals, birds, people, the church, God, and everything."

"God? What does God look like? Or maybe I don't want to know."

She laughed and said, "He looks quite human."

"Most of the pictures I've seen show Him as appearing human and usually Caucasian," I said. "Maybe you can return someday, and they can make other pictures for you."

"I hope so," she replied. "The children's lives are so hard, but they remain happy. It seems strange. Almost all American children have easier lives than these children do, but yet many of them are not happy. Why is that so? How can God let these innocent children suffer? They barely have enough to eat in a world of plenty. Some of them grow up to be good farmers or herders, and others grow up hard and cruel like the ones that killed all those people for no reason today. And yet the Bible teaches us that God is good and loving. I don't understand how He could allow that to happen."

I stared down at her for a moment. She looked like a young girl, and I wondered how she had gotten to these lonely mountains in this strange land.

"That's a question that's been debated by many people for many years," I told her.

"I know," she said still looking at me, "but what do you think?"

I thought that this is a strange night. We're trapped in an impossible situation with all our lives at risk, and I'm being asked imponderable questions as if I had the answers. Is it that way with all leaders? Maybe these questions need answering when we feel vulnerable, but that didn't mean that I had the answers.

"I believe that God gave us free will and that we can't have free will if He orders things to go a certain way," I told her. "He wants us to be happy and has given us guidance in the Bible on how to do that. If someone chooses a wrong path and threatens others, then bad things happen; but He doesn't change the bad things because then we wouldn't have free will. Often people on both sides of a war believe that God is on their side. When Christian nations fight, each thinks God is with them. He isn't on both sides, and He may help individuals in the fight but not the nations."

"I don't understand why He doesn't help the true believers."

"He could make the world perfect like heaven if He wanted, but He has chosen not to. He made the world and the universe and has chosen, for whatever reason, to give us free will to choose what path we will take. If we have free will, people may choose to do bad things; and when they do, they influence other people and their lives. If God prevented the bad things from happening, then there would not be free will," I said again.

"I suppose," Mary said. "It just doesn't seem fair."

"Life's not fair. Leave your pictures, Mary, and get in the truck," I told her. "Pray for God to help in our escape, but remember that even if we don't get away and you're killed, you'll go to heaven. That would not be so bad, would it?"

She looked up at me and smiled. "No, that wouldn't be bad."

As I left, I looked back to see Mary place several of the pictures inside her jacket and leave the rest on the ground, and I wondered why she had selected those to save. I would probably never know. Maybe she didn't know herself.

I walked back to the command area and met few people. Everyone was in the vehicles or part of the military. There was not much time left before we would need to move. I wanted to balance hitting the rebels when they were most vulnerable and getting to the airport at first light. If we were to catch the enemy asleep, it would need to be soon as I suspected these men were used to rising before dawn and would be up early even after a night of drinking. We would have to adapt the airport for a night landing and departure as it was probably only used during daylight hours normally.

When I arrived at the command area, Major Arinski with several Russian soldiers, Lieutenant Anderson, and Sergeant Davis along with a couple of Marines were already there.

"Are we ready, gentlemen?" I asked when I joined them.

"Yes, sir," answered Lieutenant Anderson. "We're prepared to move out on your command."

"All right. Let's review our status and our plan. Would you start, Major?" I said.

"Our climbers are in position and awaiting the start of our operation. It was a short and easy climb, and they have a concealed place to wait. The other group will move with us between the rebel troop camps and go behind the ridge to attack from the other side of the hilltop. I'll go with you, Colonel, with the radio operators and one guard. The remainder of my men will go with Lieutenant Anderson. Weapons are being checked and ammunition distributed now."

"Good. How about you, Lieutenant Anderson?"

"I have the main body of the men and have divided them into three groups as we planned. I will lead the group clearing the road and getting the convoy out. Lieutenant Parsky will command the second group, which will accompany the engineers to clear the main road. They'll be reinforced as soon as the trucks are beyond the enemy camp. Also they'll form the rear guard after everyone is on the road to the airport. The third group will attack the rear of the rebel force holding the road and cause as much confusion as possible. Sergeant Davis and two Marines will be with you."

"Do we have a pass word, and have all the essential papers we might have brought with us been destroyed?" I asked.

"Yes, sir. 'Key' is the pass word and the response is

'lock'. We also have some light blue material attached to our shoulders. We got that from one of the ladies who gave us her sheets. It isn't much, but it should help. As for the secret papers they were all burned this afternoon when the rebels showed up," Lieutenant Anderson said.

"Good! I don't want us to start shooting each other. There are plenty of enemy out there to do that. All right. Finish the preparations, and we'll meet in the front lines. Sergeant, will you come and get me here when we're ready to roll?" I asked.

"Yes, sir," Sergeant Davis replied.

They all saluted and left, and for the first time tonight I felt nausea and fear in the pit of my stomach. This wild plan that I had devised was going to be put into motion in the next few minutes, and for the first time in my life I was going to be in real danger. It was a feeling I had not had previously. I thought about Joy and Bobby and Maine. Would I see them again? Was I doing the right thing? What did I know? I had taken the responsibility for all of these lives as if I knew more than the United States president. If I was wrong or the plan failed, we would all be killed.

I thought about General Stratiscof and his command. They would be useful for information regarding the troop disposition, particularly for those along the road protecting his rear. We would have to get past them to reach the airport, but we didn't know their strength or position. If Stratiscof told us about them, could we trust the information? If he truly wanted us to escape, he might help us or he might try to trap us. Even if we escaped the troops facing us, could we get past the rear guard? Disaster could occur at any point. Was this a fool's plan? Maybe, but I saw no alternative.

I shook my shoulders and looked up at the trees. It was too late for doubts now. Suck it up, Colonel, I told myself. Deal with it and pretend you're a leader.

# Chapter Nineteen

The night sky was black with a myriad of stars looking just as they did in planetariums. The grass was up to our knees and rustled as we walked. I could see a few fires still glowing on the hillside across from us, but there was little noise now. I hoped they were all in an alcoholic dream world, although an occasional shadow moved against one of the fires indicating that not everyone was asleep.

I had waited about thirty minutes before Sergeant Davis returned. Now I was bent over and following Sergeant Davis closely. I almost ran into him when he stopped in a two-foot depression, which I could see was a trench once I was in it. It ran off into the darkness in both directions. Crouched over we turned to our right and walked along the trench avoiding bodies sitting or squatting along the front wall. After about fifty yards we came to a branch depression, and I could make out four dim figures sitting along the wall of the branch.

We turned into the area and sat at the end of the group.

"We are ready when you are, Colonel," said Lieutenant Anderson from among the shadows.

"Are your men ready to take out the guards?" I asked Sergeant Davis since we had not spoken after he had come to get me. "And is the civilian signal corps in position?"

"The prep team is awaiting your command," he replied. "Three of the civilians are in place, and two more will be positioned when we move out. The drivers are with their vehicles, and all the civilians including children are on board. Our troops will move forward to this side of the river with the prep team leading the way. Once the guards are removed we will cross the river and move up the hill in small groups."

It had been about 0140 hours when Sergeant Davis had gotten me at the command center, and there had been no messages from anyone. I estimated that it had taken us about ten minutes to get here. This was as good a time as any to begin.

"All right," I said, "Let's make it work."

"Yes, sir," came the reply, and the officers left.

I sat back against the edge of the trench and found Henry Jackson and John Branson next to me.

"What are you doing here?" I whispered. "I thought you were organizing the convoy with Lily."

"We are two of the signalers," Henry replied. "Lily has everything under control. She's a tiger. There won't be any problem as everyone would rather face the rebels than her anger."

There wasn't time for more conversation as Major Arinski and Sergeant Davis returned, and the line of troops in front of us began to move forward across the field like a mist. Henry, John, and I followed Sergeant Davis five yards to our right where we came to the road, which was barely visible in the darkness. Major Arinski was behind me, and he was followed by several other shadows that I presumed were his radio men.

John Branson was left hidden beside the road. He pulled his jacket tighter around his neck. It was cold despite the lack of wind.

I followed Sergeant Davis through the grass along the side of the road. Off to our left I could see vague shapes moving across the field. Halfway to the stream Henry Jackson was left huddled in the grass beside the road as John Branson had been. We proceeded for another hundred yards when Sergeant Davis signaled us to stop. I looked to our left and saw nothing moving. We waited in silence, and I felt the cold despite my thermal underwear, down jacket, and the bullet-proof vest I had on under my jacket. Lieutenant Anderson and Sergeant Davis had insisted upon my wearing the vest.

After a few intense minutes we began to move again. Following Sergeant Davis I went alongside the river until I could see the shapes ahead of us crossing the river and running through the field on the other side. The only sound that I heard was an occasional splash of water. We waited until all the troops had crossed and were climbing up the space between the two camps. Then we crossed. The rocky river bed made walking hazardous and slow. Fortunately, the water wasn't deep, but I found that it was cold when a little ran down inside my right boot.

As I ran across the field, the grass and roots grabbed at my boots, and I stumbled several times but did not fall. I was breathing heavily and my chest ached when we reached the base of the hill. In the grass to our right were three bodies lying on top of each other like a marker. In the dark I couldn't see any of their wounds or weapons. Without pausing Sergeant Davis continued up the hill into the tree line where we passed several of our men holding their weapons at the ready and watching the camps on either side. However, there was little activity in the camps, and no one appeared to have noticed us.

I seemed to be the only one with fatigue and had no choice except to force myself to continue to climb after Sergeant Davis. Major Arinski and his men were behind me. The guards had folded in behind them like stalking wolves. About halfway up what appeared to me to be Mount Everest we stopped, and Sergeant Davis pointed to the clearing to our left. I could see the hut through the trees. No one was between us and the open area. There was a dim, flickering light coming from the only window on our side of the hut, but it gave little illumination beyond the wall of the structure. I couldn't see a door. It must have faced down the hill away from us.

Suddenly two of the Marines who had been following us came up, handed their weapons to Sergeant Davis, and disappeared into the shadows. The rest of the group formed a semicircle below and to either side of us. We waited quietly. I heard a couple of dull thuds followed by silence, and after a moment Sergeant Davis signaled Major Arinski and his men to go on to the hut.

We trailed after the Russians and on reaching the hut went around to the door, which was closed. As I came up to the door, I noted a body on either side of the entryway. Major Arinski and his men, along with the Marines, had gone inside, and I followed with Sergeant Davis, who was carrying the Marines' weapons.

At that moment the fireworks began. There was heavy firing off to our right and it spread quickly across the hilltop to our left and to the rocky promontory as our troops fired into the enemy camps. The rebels must have been surprised because I was, despite knowing that it was coming.

The cacophony increased rapidly, and I could smell smoke and fire. The gates of hell had been opened.

The shepherd's shack had thin walls that were little more than wind breaks. There was one room divided into two areas by a half wall with an old wood burning stove at one end and its pipe going through the ceiling. The stove heated both areas and had a steaming pot on it when we entered. Both rooms were lit with gas lanterns and a couple of large flashlights. The left section was the larger of the two areas, and there was a small table against the outside wall with a lantern hanging above it. The table held a radio and scattered papers. In front of the table one of the Russian soldiers was sitting on a three-legged stool and speaking into the microphone. The bodies of three rebel soldiers were spilling their blood onto the dirt floor in the center of the room, and their rifles were leaning against the far wall. At the near end of the half wall a Russian soldier held his Uzi while watching both rooms.

The fighting was becoming heavier, and the noise from the mortar and small weapons fire was deafening. The fresh cool air was contaminated with the acrid smell of smoke that was wafting through the woods and fields. The fighting was occurring not just in the middle of the encampment but also up on the ridge where the Russian mountaineers had scaled the cliff as well as across the valley where I hoped Lieutenant Anderson was opening the road. The night was ablaze with fireworks and streaks of light that I could see through the window and door. Occasional rounds came through the walls of the shack, but they were mostly spent. I thought this was dangerous, but I was too occupied to be afraid. It would have been beautiful if it wasn't so terrifying. I felt excited and yet calm. Everything seemed to move in slow motion.

The area to my right contained a small table in the center with two wooden chairs on either side and two bed rolls on the floor next to the wall. General Stratiscof, whom I recognized from his pictures, lay on one of the bed rolls wearing his blue military pants and a blood-stained dirty white undershirt. He appeared short in stature with a round clean-shaven face and uncombed long dark hair. He was pressing on his abdomen, and there was obvious agony on his face.

The other man was a dark-skinned, bearded Arab wearing a dirt-stained white robe. His face was thin and his beard was long, gray, and unkempt. He was seated on one of the chairs with his hands on the table and looking at the general. Our arrival had been a surprise.

I walked into the right side of the room and left the management of the command center to Major Arinski. There were papers and leftover food scattered across the tabletop. Although I couldn't read the Russian or Arabic or whatever language in which the papers were written, I thought they might be of importance and stuffed them into my backpack.

"Who are you and where is your commanding officer?" asked General Stratiscof grimacing in pain.

"I am Colonel Jacoby," I told him. "I apologize for my dress, but my uniform is not back from the tailor."

I put my backpack on over my scruffy jacket. I obviously did not appear to be a Marine colonel.

"You are the new commander of the refugees? I thought we were under attack by an American rescue mission, although I didn't think the American president would interfere. He is stretched too thin to send much of a force and wouldn't want to risk it anyway. He was easy to convince. But how did you get here? Who are these men attacking us?" the general asked.

"Just the troops we had available. We weren't waiting for you to murder us as you did the other refugee group yesterday afternoon," I replied.

"I told your president that I would let you go in the morning."

"You lied and the president had to believe you. We didn't. You were there at the massacre and did nothing to stop it. And it was a massacre," I told him.

After a sigh he said, "I would have prevented it if I could have. There was nothing I could do. It was certainly not to my advantage, particularly killing the ambassador and his family. War is war."

"You are responsible for this one," I answered.

He nodded and pleaded, "I am in terrible pain. I will not recover from this wound without medical treatment, which is not available here. Please don't leave me to die slowly."

"I understand your problem, general. I will see what we can do for you before we leave."

At that moment Major Arinski interrupted to tell me that the rebel commander on the right side of the road was asking for orders. I told him to have the commander order his troops to attack our position across the stream but to keep to the side of the valley as all the troops would be moving forward.

"Do you want us to contact the Uzbek men to move forward now?" the major asked.

"No. Wait until our convoy has crossed to this side of the river before moving them forward. Besides, I hope they will fight the other tribes and keep everyone occupied," I said.

There were flashes of light on the other side of the river among the rebel forces. I presumed that these were mortar rounds from the Russian troops on the hilltop. Apparently that part of the operation was a success, but most urgent was the opening of the road by Lieutenant Anderson's men.

Time was important. What was happening?

# Chapter Twenty

Joy sent Bobby outside to play while she cooked dinner. She had been crying intermittently all afternoon.
She told herself that crying did no good and would upset Bobby if he saw her, but she didn't seem to be able
to help herself. Every so often she just found herself in
tears and feeling lonely and afraid.

Her mother had called from her home in Quincy,
Massachusetts, where Joy had spent her childhood.
Joy remembered the old brown-shingled two-story
house three blocks from the beach. She remembered
her room with the single bed, the bureau of oak painted
white, the small mirror above it, the old red leather
chair, and the book shelves with all her dolls; and she

reflected back on her life growing up there. There were the Sunday dinners after church with her parents, Aunt Jane, Uncle Tony, and her sister, Martha. Her mother had always cooked a leg of lamb, broiled potatoes, and green beans. It was a tradition that never seemed to vary except for a rare weekend trip.

The family had gone for weekends in New Hampshire to ski in the winter and to hike and to swim in the lake in the summer, but there was no reason to travel when you lived at a vacation destination. Although most of the year was cold and spent in school, Joy's childhood summers had been at the beach, and she had loved it even though the water was cold and the beach rocky. Of course, as a teenager she had worked in the Sea Gift store selling shells, shell jewelry, and other mementos to tourists. Looking back it had been a fun life, and it had seemed as safe and solid as the New England coast.

Joy had let the answering machine pick up the calls all afternoon, and she had answered her mother's call only when she recognized her mother's voice. Joy's sister, Martha, had told her mother about Robert's appointment as colonel, and her mother had all the usual questions to which Joy had no answers. Her mother had wanted to come to Maine to stay with her, but Joy had told her that she was fine and would keep in touch.

Joy had watched the news continuously, but there was nothing new about Robert. It was night there, and nothing was expected to happen until morning. The commentators repeated the same opinions as earlier in the day. The optimistic ones and those favoring the administration were sure all would be well if the refugees followed the president's orders to surrender; the pessimistic ones and those critical of the president predicted disaster.

When the timer went off Joy called Bobby in to wash his hands for dinner. She took the chicken from the oven, fixed the potatoes and beans, and served two plates for Bobby and herself. She put them on the kitchen table and Bobby sat down at one place. Joy stood behind her chair and said a brief prayer blessing the food and asking for Robert's safe return.

As she sat down, the phone rang again. After the third ring the answering machine answered and a female voice said, "This is the State Department office of Under Secretary, Mr. Harold Johnson. If you are there, Mrs. Jacoby, please answer. Mr. Johnson would like a word with you. I am not a reporter."

Joy stood, went to the phone, and picked it up.

"This is Mrs. Jacoby." she said.

"Please hold for Mr. Johnson," came the reply.

After a moment Mr. Johnson said, "This is Harold Johnson at the State Department, Mrs. Jacoby. As you know, your husband has been put in command of the troops protecting the refugees in Uzbekistan. This was done at the request of the leaders of the group, but we don't know why this request was made. Have you heard from him or do you know why this request was made?"

Joy took a moment to collect her thoughts. It was obvious that the government had no clue about what was happening or at least didn't want to admit that they did.

"I've not heard from Robert for about a week," she told him. "He told me then that the foreign personnel in the area and the clinic were being evacuated, and that he would be leaving in the second group as he was trying to set up the clinic to operate without medical oversight. I haven't heard from him since then." She paused and then said, "You must know what is happening better than I do. I only know what is reported on the news, and I presume that you have other sources of information."

"The president has been assured by General Stratiscof that all of the foreigners including the military will be released in the morning. We are concerned that your husband will try something foolish and cause a massacre. Would you be willing to speak with him?"

"I have no way of reaching him unless you do, and why would you need me to speak to him? You could tell him anything he needed to know," Joy replied. "Do you believe General Stratiscof?"

"He will need our help if he is successful in his war. He would not want to antagonize us, and there's no reason for him to want to hurt the refugees," Johnson said.

"Are we not antagonized by the murder of the Americans today?"

"As you well know from the news reports that incident was caused by a small group of Stratiscof's army. We believe that he will let the Americans and Russians go in the morning as promised. All our experts agree. But this is only true if there is no attempt to escape or if there is no surrender, and we have relayed this information to Colonel Jacoby. We hoped that you would be more persuasive than we are."

"I have no way to reach him," Joy replied. "And even if I did I would have to rely on his judgment as he is actually there. I know only what's on the news and what you tell me."

"I understand, Mrs. Jacoby. I feel certain that all will be well. I will keep you informed if I have any news."

"Thank you," Joy said and hung up the phone. However, she did not feel comforted as she joined Bobby for dinner.

# Chapter Twenty-One

The smoke and noise seemed to increase, but that may have been my imagination. I was in command and had no clue as to what was happening outside of this room. What a way to run a battle. I wondered if all commanders in a fight faced this problem.

As I turned back to the table, I considered General Stratiscof's request. It was obvious that we could not take prisoners nor could we afford to leave commanders in place to organize pursuit. Even tying them up would not be adequate as rebel soldiers would come here soon to check on their commanders and would free them. Killing them was the only option, and it should be done soon. It was also apparent that I would be the one to kill them. I could not delegate all the unpleasant business to subordinates as I would appear weak to the soldiers I led. I was neither afraid nor excited by the prospect. I had never killed anyone, and my life had been dedicated to healing and preserving life, but it had to be done, and I was the one to do it. It was war, and it was not glorious or wonderful. It was dirty hard work that altered the participants. This was about surviving. I could and would do this even though I had no desire to do it. I would be changed as all people involved in conflict were changed. A decent person has a difficult time dealing with killing another person, even an enemy combatant, but I would have to deal with all that later.

My thoughts were interrupted when Major Arinski entered the room and said. "Lieutenant Anderson has reported that the road is open and the trucks are moving. We should leave in the next few minutes."

"Noted," I replied. "Order the rebel forces on the far side of the river to begin to move forward but to stay out of the center of the valley. Prepare to destroy this shack and equipment. And get a sharp knife or machete for me."

"Yes, sir," he replied and left the room.

"Americans frequently amaze me with their ingenuity. You have taken us by surprise, and I hope that you are successful in escaping," the bearded man said in excellent English and without fear. "It was not part of my plan to destroy the Western refugees, but it may be advantageous in the end. Allah guides all these events."

"Who are you and what is it that you want to accomplish besides the defeat of the government?" I asked.

"I'm not important and overthrowing the government is not as important as getting American and other Western troops out of Uzbekistan, particularly American," he replied.

"You expect to win a victory over NATO armies? Iraq has not been a success for you. Much of the country is stable."

"On the contrary," he answered. "Iraq is proving successful, and I hope for equal success here. Did you think we thought that we could beat you militarily? There is little chance of that. After all, it may have taken sixty years or more, but the Soviet Union was defeated financially not militarily. With little expense we have caused billions of dollars a year to be spent in Iraq, and with a few radio messages we can get America to spend millions of dollars in security. Look at your national debt with much of it owed to foreign countries. We are patient, and the collapse will come. I may not see it, but that will not stop the cause. We have planned for my death for sometime. Actually I thought it would have occurred before now."

"You will meet your god today."

"So be it," he said.

I took out my pistol and walked behind the bearded man who remained seated at the table. He didn't move. I placed the barrel against the back of this head.

"Praise be to Allah!" he shouted and I pulled the trigger.

It was done. He slumped forward into the table, and a small pool of blood formed under his head. I felt nothing.

I went to where General Stratiscof lay on the bed roll and stood over him.

"Put your shirt over your face," I ordered.

He reached up with his right hand and pulled the shirt up over his face keeping his left hand on his wounded abdomen. "Thank you," he said.

Major Arinski returned as I fired through the shirt. I turned, slipped off my backpack, and placed it on the edge of the table. I found the plastic bag in the side pocket with half of a sandwich in it, discarded the half sandwich, and gave the bag to Major Arinski.

"Cut off one of this gentleman's fingers and seal it in the bag, please," I asked.

Using the large knife that he had in his hand he easily cut off the index finger of the left hand of the bearded corpse. He put the finger in the bag and handed it back to me. I sealed it and put it back in the side pocket of my pack.

Sergeant Davis entered and told us that the convoy had arrived and was proceeding up the road. Part of Lieutenant Anderson's force was moving out ahead of the convoy trucks and would join the troops we had sent to scout the road further on.

"We are prepared to burn this hut, and we need to leave now, Colonel," he said.

"In a moment," I said. "Major Arinski, have the radio man order the rebel force guarding the main road junction to move a half mile north on the road and to prepare for an attacking force from that direction. Tell them that Stratiscof is moving toward the airport with some of his troops. What about the climbers?"

"That's been accomplished as we planned," he replied. "The climbers and the assisting team will move behind the camp and meet us further up the road."

"Excellent," I said. "Let's go catch our bus."

We left the hut and ran up the hill toward the trees. Smoke made the scene hazy, and gunfire was everywhere. Flashes from the gun barrels appeared in the haze like brief match lights in the dark. The sound was deafening, but I could hear occasional bullets buzzing near me. As before, I followed Sergeant Davis closely and hoped he knew where he was going.

When we reached the tree line, the hut burst into flame behind us. I could see several men running up toward us from the hut. Suddenly the last figure dropped. The first man looked back, hesitated, then crouched and went back. He grabbed the jacket of the figure below him and dragged him into the tree line.

Sergeant Davis moved into the trees and turned right down a rocky gulley toward the road. As I turned I looked across the valley to where we had been camped and could see flashes of gunfire. The gunfire behind us became heavier as the hut burned brightly. I hoped that the enemy was as confused as I was.

I moved as quickly as I could under the trees trying to avoid rocks, roots, and low tree limbs in the dark. There was little brush in the gulley, but the ground was uneven. At least we weren't running uphill any longer, and I had a chance to catch my breath. I was breathing heavily and my chest hurt, but there wasn't time to rest. I wished that I had been in better physical condition. I had always thought that I was in good shape. I was wrong.

After a few minutes we came to the dirt road where a culvert passed beneath it. Across the road I could see the outline of the trucks.

Sergeant Davis nudged me and said, "Get in the first truck. Major Arinski and his men can ride in the back. The other vehicles are for Lieutenant Anderson's men."

I ran across the road and in front of the first truck. I opened the door to get in and was surprised to see that the driver was Lily Blackthorne.

"What are you doing here?" I asked her.

"I have experience driving trucks and can drive as well as a man. We needed drivers, and I was a logical choice," she answered.

I nodded and walked to the rear of the truck as the Russians came running across the road and climbed in the back of the truck. The firing and noise was a little behind us and off to our left, but there were sporadic shots in the trees above the road. The noise from the main camp was partially blocked by the hillside.

One of the last of the men to cross the road stumbled and fell. I hadn't heard or seen a shot; before I could move, a figure from the vehicle behind us ran to the fallen man and attempted to get him up.

There were more shots now, and I saw that they were coming from among the trees about a third of the way up the hill. Bullets were hitting the road and around the truck, and I ducked behind the rear wheel.

Two of the men who were standing at the back of the truck with me turned and ran back to aid their fallen comrade. They took over from the man who had gone first, and they lifted the wounded man by his arms and dragged him to the back of our truck. The injured man screamed in pain as several men reached out from the truck, caught him under his shoulders, and pulled him into the vehicle.

The fire from the hillside was almost continuous now, but I couldn't see where the shots were going. From the far side of the road, where several men were crouching along the bank, came answering automatic weapons fire that sprayed the area where the shooter had been. After a few moments the firing stopped, and all was silent on our side of the hill.

I moved to the rear of the truck and asked, "How is he?"

There was a moment of confusion and then someone answered "He is shot in the shoulder. We'll take care of him for now."

As I turned, I noticed that the figure in the road was on his hands and knees crawling toward us. I sprinted out and knelt by his side.

"Please help me. I've been hit in my leg."

It wasn't a man at all, and I recognized the voice.

"Dorothy, it's Dr. Jacoby."

"Is it really you, Robert?" she asked.

"Yes," I replied. "Will you show me where your wound is?"

She sat back on the dirt and pointed to her left thigh, but in the dark I couldn't see anything except for a dark spot on her pants.

I picked her up under her arms and knees and carried her to the tailgate of the truck. Fortunately, she was not heavy.

I asked for a flashlight, which was passed back. Someone shone the light on her leg as I cut her pants with a penknife to reveal the wound. There was some blood, but no major arteries appeared to have been damaged.

Sergeant Davis came to the rear of truck and said, "Colonel, we need to go. We still have to get past the armies on the main road. They won't wait long before coming to investigate what's happening."

"I know, Sergeant. Give me a couple of minutes."

"Yes, sir," he said, and he returned to the cab of the truck.

I placed my folded handkerchief over the wound and bound it with her scarf. It was tight enough to hold the bandage in place but not cut off the circulation.

I took her hand and said to her, "I think you'll be fine. It's mostly a flesh wound, and we should be at a hospital before any infection sets in. You were very brave to try to help that man."

"Thank you, Robert," she said in a small voice. "Will he be all right?"

"I think so," I told her and asked the men to make room for her.

They moved up and made a space for her on the floor, but there wasn't enough space for both of us. I helped move her onto the area on the floor, closed the tailgate, and went around to the front of the truck.

"All right, Sergeant, get us out of here," I ordered as I got in the cab and closed the door.

"Move ahead and try to catch up with the rest of our convoy," he said to Lily, and she put the truck into gear and began moving forward slowly.

Behind us several trucks started up also. Lieutenant Anderson's troops must be pulling out, I thought. We moved slowly up the road as it was difficult to see the road in the dark, and we were not using headlights. Lily was staring ahead concentrating on the road.

"Did all the trucks get through?" I asked her.

"I don't know. I think so," she replied without looking up from the road. "This is the ninth truck. All those in front of me made it through, but some of them were hit by fire. I don't know if anyone was hurt. When the shooting started, it was like an explosion with firing everywhere within seconds. I started my engine when the shooting began, as we had been instructed. In less than five minutes the truck in front of me began to move forward. The flashlight worked well, and I stayed close to him. As we went across the valley, I saw some firing at the trucks ahead of me, but it didn't last long as there was almost immediate return fire from our troops along the road. I think the rear of my truck was hit a couple of times or at least it sounded that way. It seemed to take forever to get across the river and beyond their encampment. We were moving so slowly. But it probably didn't take but a few minutes. When I got to the spot you found me, a Marine signaled me to pull to the side and stop. At least I wasn't being shot at, and then you came. The whole trip couldn't have lasted more than ten minutes or so, but it seemed like a lifetime."

She told me all of this without taking her eyes off the road.

Suddenly there were figures running across the road just ahead of us, and Lily jammed on the brakes. Sergeant Davis took his weapon and dropped to the ground next to the truck. He tapped on the truck and several men got out of the back. They walked ahead, and I could barely see them in the dark. After a few moments Sergeant Davis signaled Lily to move ahead.

When we got to him, Sergeant Davis got into the slowly-moving vehicle and told us that these were the Russian troops from the hilltop. He instructed Lily to stop in the midst of the men so they could get in the trucks.

"Will we have enough room for them in these trucks?" I asked.

"We will cram them in," he said. "We don't have far to go, and I don't know if all the trucks behind us made it."

"Good decision, Sergeant," I said.

We started off again and the night was quiet ahead of us, which was a good sign. We had to get onto the main road without fighting a major battle.

# Chapter Twenty-Two

After she and Bobby finished eating, Joy cleared the table and washed the dishes. Bobby watched cartoons until his bedtime at eight o'clock when Joy bathed him and put him in bed. He said his prayers including asking for protection for his father, and Joy tucked him in and kissed him goodnight.

She went downstairs and turned on the television. The stock market was down moderately in active trading mostly over the worry about the rebel activity in Uzbekistan. The president had promised an investigation into the murders of the Westerners by the rebel force, but there was nothing new on Robert or the second group of refugees. It was night there, and apparently there had been no communication since the evening before. No one expected any action until morning. It was felt that the trapped refugees had no way of escape and would surrender, be attacked, or left alone in the morning.

Joy thought that it was strange that there had been no word from the Americans, although this had been explained by the lack of electrical power and the need to save on their batteries. She was sure that Robert would contact her if he could. She turned the television off intending to read a magazine when there was a knock at the door.

It was Janet and her husband, Jack. Joy let them in.

"We came over to keep you company," Janet said. "It isn't good to be alone during times of stress, and we brought some hot chocolate and snacks."

"That's very nice of you," Joy said closing the door behind them.

She led them to the kitchen table and then got out three mugs. Janet put the thermos and bags of potato chips and pretzels on the table. Jack and Janet took off their coats, and Jack hung them over the fourth chair. Janet produced a small bag of marshmallows, put a few in each mug, and poured the hot chocolate from her thermos into the mugs.

"Have you heard anymore news?" she asked Joy.

"Not really," Joy replied. "Someone from the State Department called to ask me to contact Robert, but I think they wanted to know if I knew anything that they didn't."

"Well, there should be some news shortly as it must be getting near dawn there," Jack said. "Whatever is going to happen will probably occur early in the morning."

Joy sipped her hot chocolate and wondered if Janet and Jack had come to keep her company or to learn the latest news. Then she thought that was an unkind and unneighborly thought. All her friends and family were very solicitous, but Joy felt some of them were waiting for the worst to happen. Of course, the television news and commentators were also expecting the worst. Maybe everyone, even the government, was expecting a disaster. No one seemed optimistic no matter how encouraging they tried to be.

"Yes," Joy said. "We should have some news in the next few hours. I haven't heard from Robert in the last several days so I'm at least glad to know that he's alive. Something must have happened to his phone or he would have called me."

"I'm sure he would," Janet replied. "Would you like to play cards or just talk? We are here to do whatever you want."

"I don't think that I could concentrate on cards," Joy said. "But I appreciate the company."

There was silence for a few minutes while everyone drank some of their chocolate. Then Jack asked, "Did Robert have any military experience to qualify for his appointment as colonel in the Marines? I don't remember him talking about it if he did."

"Not that I know about. He was in the military, the army I think, after the Vietnam War. He served as an enlisted man since he hadn't been to medical school. I don't think he had any experience as an officer."

"That's interesting," Jack commented. "I wonder why he was put in command."

"No one seems to know, not even the president. One of the government's concerns is that he would do something that would interfere with the surrender that's been arranged."

"What did you tell them?" Janet asked.

"I told them that I wasn't there and that Robert would have to make up his own mind. After all, he is on the spot and knows more about what's happening than I do. What else could I tell them?"

Just then the phone rang, and Joy jumped. The phone had been relatively quiet for the past few hours as Joy had not taken any calls, and she thought it might be Robert or some news about him since, as Jack had pointed out, it was nearing morning where Robert was. The answering machine had proved its worth today, and Joy let it answer once more.

This time it was her mother again, and Joy picked up the phone. Her mother was worried since there was nothing new on the television reports, and she wanted to know if Joy had heard anything and how she was doing. Joy told her that she was fine and about the call from the State Department. After some discussion about visiting and Joy explaining that she needed to stay where she was in case Robert called, her mother agreed and hung up with Joy's promise to call when she learned anything.

Joy returned to Jack and Janet and was pleased that she didn't have to wait alone as her anxiety was overwhelming.

# Chapter Twenty-Three

We passed the entrance to the vodka plant and approached the main road, which was wider, better maintained, but still gravel. It occurred to me that we could be fired on by the rebel troops guarding the road or by our own forces that had preceded us. Not very reassuring thoughts it seemed to me.

Sergeant Davis told Lily to stop the truck a couple of hundred yards short of the main road junction, and he got out and went up the road with three men from the back of our vehicle. They stayed on the side of the road and soon disappeared into the darkness.

Although there was still considerable noise from the battle behind us, it was reduced from the previous levels and more tolerable. I could see flashes of light in the side mirror, and the whole area behind us seemed hazy like a low cloud reflecting light from a small village. It was surreal as was the whole night, but so far we had done well. The price paid for our success this far was unknown.

After a few minutes someone came up to Lily's window and told her to go on slowly and to turn right on the main road.

As we approached the junction I could see two trucks across the road to our left with a number of figures around them. We made the turn slowly, and Sergeant Davis joined us.

"Keep moving," he instructed Lily, "so that the trucks behind us can get through."

"What's happening? Where's the rebel force?" I asked him.

"The rebels are camped about a mile down the road," he answered. "We were able to eliminate the three guards that had been left here without arousing the rest of the force. Two members of our advance force have been wounded but none seriously, and none have been killed. We've placed mines across the road a few yards away from us. The rest of the group has gone ahead to find a place to provide cover for our retreat. We'll have to regroup when we reach the airport."

"Do we know how far the airport is?" I asked.

"According to the map it's in a field off to our left about five miles down the road. The river on our left here crosses the road a couple of miles further along. It appears to be fairly wide. We can blow the bridge and set up a rear guard action there until we can get the civilians and the main part of our force out by plane."

"Who has our radio?" I asked.

"Jonsey has it in one of the jeeps behind us. He'll meet us on the other side of the bridge. The trucks with the civilians and four Marine guards have gone on to the airport. We don't expect any resistance there."

"I hope not," I replied. "We're spread thin as it is. As soon as we know what kind of airport we have, I would like to bring the planes in. The sooner we're out of here the better. It won't take long for the rebel commanders to figure out what's happened, and those troops on the road behind us may come after us."

"Yes, sir," Davis said.

Lily turned on the truck lights and drove rapidly along the road raising a cloud of dust behind us. I could see only the hazy outline of the vehicle immediately following us, but his headlights showed where he was. The area to our left appeared open with an occasional line of trees. It was still too dark to make out any images in the field, and the river wasn't visible. The black sky with a myriad of stars covered the area like a dome and made it seem enclosed.

To our right was the dark shape of trees coming close to the road, which was flat and could be seen only a few yards ahead.

We rode in silence except for the engine roar and the rattle of the truck body. We crossed a small metal bridge with a cement surface. It was about twenty yards long, and there was a figure standing in the road on the other end. Lily slowed down and stopped at the end of the bridge where Sergeant Davis got out and went to confer with the man in front of us. He then went to the truck behind us and spoke to them briefly.

Three trucks passed us before Sergeant Davis waved a covered jeep to pull to the right side of the road in front of us. Two more trucks passed before Lily pulled in behind the jeep. I noticed bullet holes in the canvas and bodies of the last two trucks, and one was leaking oil or gas onto the road.

Lieutenant Anderson came up to my window and told me that Jonsey had the radio in the jeep. Fortunately it had not been damaged in the fighting.

"Who's in charge here?" I asked.

"One of the civilian engineers has placed C-4 on this side of the bridge and thinks that he can bring it down," replied Sergeant Davis, "but no one has organized a defensive position."

I got out of the truck and walked with Sergeant Davis and Lieutenant Anderson toward the jeep. I noticed that in the heat of action saluting had been discarded, and this was fine with me.

"Lieutenant, would you organize a rear guard action and destroy the bridge after all our forces have crossed?" I asked.

"Yes, sir," he replied and saluted.

So much for saluting I thought.

"Take only as many men as you need and the trucks needed to carry them," I ordered returning his salute. "Sergeant Davis, get the engineers and some explosives to mine the road alongside the airport. Leave a means of communication with Lieutenant Anderson."

Lieutenant Anderson and Sergeant Davis left, and I sat down in the front seat of the jeep. Jonsey was in the back seat with the radio beside him, and an armed

Marine was in the driver's seat. A moment later Lily's truck with the Russians in the rear drove past us.

I turned to Jonsey and asked if he could get the navy planes for me.

"Yes, sir," he replied. "It will only take a minute. We've been in contact with them as they wanted to know what was going on."

I turned back and looked down the road. The area, where the rebel camp had been, appeared still like a distant storm with flashes of lightning and a continuous dull roar. Five or six more trucks and vehicles rolled by in a cloud of choking dust. Two of them stopped further down the road, and their drivers and occupants ran back to join the men that Lieutenant Anderson was stationing at the end of the bridge and along the river bank.

Jonsey nudged me and handed me the phone. "Lieutenant Commander Robertson," he said.

I took the phone and said, "This is Colonel Jacoby. We're about a mile or two from the airport, and I hope to be ready for pickup in twenty or thirty minutes. Some of our forces are on their way to the airport now. How far away are you?"

"We're twenty minutes from you," came the reply. "We'll move closer but need to stay in international air space until you're ready. Understand the urgency. Call when you are at the airport and ready to board. Out."

I handed the phone back to Jonsey and walked to where Lieutenant Anderson was overseeing the defense of the river bank and the bridge.

"Do you have everything you need?" I asked him.

"Yes, sir. I think so," he replied. "We should have

enough ammunition and fire power to hold out for awhile."

"Good."

"The Russian troops holding the main road have said they think the last of our vehicles have passed. About six vehicles are missing, but there were nine additional trucks taken from the rebels. There's been no traffic on the road for the last eight minutes. As you can tell from here, there's still a lot of firing in the enemy camp but that's probably the rebels fighting each other. Do you want the Russians to pull out?" Lieutenant Anderson asked.

"All right," I said. "Have them form a skirmish line about a quarter of a mile up the road from here. That will slow down any pursuit and give you warning before they reach you. They may not chase us as we have no military value, but we can't count on that. Their whole attitude is difficult to explain. If you don't need them, the Russians can join us at the airport."

"Yes, sir," he replied.

"We'll have rear guard forces on the road outside the airport to help cover your withdrawal. Keep in touch."

Yes, sir," he said and saluted.

I returned the salute and went back to the jeep.

"Let's move on to the airport," I said.

The jeep moved along quickly, but not quietly, on the gravel road, which was now surrounded by fields. I couldn't see any trees or hills on either side. We seemed to be all alone in an empty space. But we weren't alone, as someone appeared out of the darkness just ahead of us, and beyond him on the left were lights and the outline of a small building.

We stopped next to the figure who turned out to be a Marine, and he looked in the car window.

"Colonel Jacoby? We've been expecting you," he said. "Sergeant Davis told us he would meet you in front of the hangar, which is that small building ahead of us. The entry road is on the left in front of the building. There isn't much here."

"Thank you," I replied, and we proceeded to the gate and up to the building.

Sergeant Davis and Major Arinski were outside the entrance to the hangar, which was a one-story cinder block structure with slanted shingled roof and about a hundred feet long and half that wide. It appeared to be unpainted. The landing strip was just beyond the building and stretched down the field parallel to the main road. The only thing separating the road and the strip was fifty or so yards of unmowed grass and a drainage ditch next to the road.

We stopped next to Sergeant Davis, and I got out to speak to Major Arinski.

"Where are your men, Major?"

"Most of the men from the hilltop are here, sir. Some are working on defending the landing strip and a few are with Lieutenant Anderson."

"How many have we lost?" I asked.

"I don't know for certain, but would guess about five or more killed and another ten wounded. It could have been much worse. The wounded are in the hangar where there is a little light. They are being cared for by a couple of nurses and some of the women."

I turned to Sergeant Davis and asked him the same question.

"As you know," he said, "we have some personnel along the road at the bridge with Lieutenant Anderson, and some across the bridge. Some are setting up defensive positions on the road opposite the strip, and some are here. There are a number of wounded and at least twelve dead. There are four civilians dead and two wounded."

"I'm sorry about the dead and wounded," I replied. "I presume there are no landing lights."

"No, sir," he said. "I've sent vehicles to light the beginning of the runway and as much of the rest as possible. There are a few spotlights on the roof of the hangar to light this end of the strip and the loading area. Fortunately, the runway is paved, but it's less than a mile long. There's room for two planes at this end, but one would have to park in the gravel space."

"All right," I said. "Get the wounded and the civilians ready to board. I'm going to bring the planes in now. Put the bodies on the second plane and make sure we fill the plane before it leaves."

I told Jonsey to get Commander Robertson for me. As he worked the radio there were two distant explosions followed by rapid gunfire from the way we had come. The pursuit had apparently begun.

Jonsey handed me the phone as Sergeant Davis spoke to a Marine who had come from the building.

"Commander Robertson," I said into the phone. "We're ready for you to pick us up."

"Roger that, Colonel," came the reply. "What is your situation?"

"Peaceful at the moment," I said, "but I expect that to change quickly. I think the enemy is attacking our rear guard now. I don't know the enemy size or how long we can hold. How soon can you be here?"

"We're coming now and our ETA is fifteen minutes. What's the field like?"

"The field is one paved strip, less than a mile long and lighted by truck lights," I told him. "We should be able to load two planes at a time."

"There are three of us. Can we get in and load at the same time?"

"Probably not," I replied. "For one thing the area is small, and two we have to defend the strip while the first planes load and leave. We can mine the road and create some diversions for getting the last plane out, but that will be the most hazardous flight."

"Roger that. Be ready to load as soon as we land."

"Roger. Look forward to seeing you. Out."

I returned the phone to Jonsey and found Sergeant Davis waiting to speak to me. As I suspected, the enemy had found that we had escaped and were in pursuit.

"There were about twenty-five men in two trucks, and they've been destroyed with grenade launchers," he told me. "They're most likely from the force guarding the road. We can probably expect a much larger force shortly. The skirmishers have moved up the road a bit and will try to hold the next force for awhile before retreating to the bridge. We aren't going to have much time."

"Can we hold them beyond the airport?" I asked.

"Our best chance is at the river," he said. "Lieutenant Anderson will blow the bridge and that should slow them down. However, there may be other places to cross."

"We'll need to hold them beyond the other end of

the runway in order to get our planes off. Is there a fuel truck here and does it have aviation fuel in it?"

"I believe so, but I don't know how much gas it has."

"Find out," I ordered. "If there's enough fuel spread it across the grassy area between the road and the airstrip. We can use it as a smoke screen when we take off. There isn't much wind so hopefully it won't blow back over the airstrip. If there's enough, fill up the ditch along the road as well."

"Yes, sir."

Then I asked Major Arinski to get the Russian military ready to help load the moment the planes stopped.

"Put the civilians on the first plane, and if there's still room load the wounded. Load any leftover civilians and wounded on the second plane before loading the military. Are there any dead bodies?" I asked.

"Yes, sir. But I don't know how many," he said.

"I'm not familiar with these craft, but if they have cargo space, put the bodies in there. If not, find some spot for them if you can. The planes will arrive in approximately fifteen minutes. Be ready to load."

"Yes, sir," he said and went into the hangar.

As I had nothing else to do at the moment, I decided to check on the wounded to see if I could help. I went toward the small door in the side of the building when Roger Taylor caught up to me.

"Excuse me, Colonel," he said. "May I send my story now that we're safely away from the rebel force? I have it written, and it can be sent quickly."

"I'll ask Sergeant Davis to give you your equipment. Do you need to be on the ground to send it?"

"I already have all that I need except your permission."

It occurred to me that I should contact Admiral Clark before any story appeared in the press, so I told him that he could fly out on the last plane and file his story after the first two planes had left.

"Thank you," he said.

"Thank you for keeping your promise. I think you can count on having a scoop on this story."

"No question about that. By the way, a Dorothy Roberts was asking about you. She is among the wounded in the hangar. I think she was shot in the leg. If you have a moment, you may want to speak to her."

"Thanks. I'll try to find her," I told him.

I went back to Jonsey and asked him to get Admiral Clark for me. As I looked down the road, I could see that there was more fighting going on, but I could not tell if it was at the river.

Jonsey handed me the speaker and said, "It's Admiral Clark."

"I am sorry to get you up so early, sir," I said. "However, I thought it was important to let you know what was happening."

"Thank you," he replied. "I was up anyway, and I gather from the radio conversations that you're at the airport."

"As you said, we're at the airport but are being pursued. We've taken some casualties, but I don't know how many. Briefly, we attacked the rebel forces between the two rebel camps and then came in behind the rebel troops to get the road cleared long enough for the trucks and civilians to escape. We also destroyed their headquarters and their commanders who were in them. Most of our troops are at the airport, but some of our force is providing rear guard protection at the river. Lieutenant Anderson is in command of that group. There appears to be fighting occurring there, but I have no further information on that. I expect the planes to arrive in the next few minutes. Also the story will be released through CNN by Roger Taylor, who's with us."

"I appreciate your informing me before the media gets the story. The Pentagon will want to know before the public does. When you say the commanders are dead, are you referring to General Stratiscof?"

"Yes. The general and another man with him were killed. I don't know who the other man was, but he seemed to be someone of importance, although he didn't appear to be part of the military force," I told him.

"I know you are busy. Call me when you are all out and give me a more complete report. Good luck."

I returned the phone to Jonsey and looked down the road to where the sounds of combat were increasing. I noticed that the distant end of the runway was lighted by headlights, and as I watched, other headlights lit up the other parts of the strip. Much of the strip was dark, but there was enough light to see where the runway was located. I didn't hear any plane engines, but they were probably too far away.

I decided that I still had time to visit the wounded and get some idea of the number of casualties before the planes arrived.

There was a door and a single window in the side of the building that faced the open area in which I was standing. I went through the doorway into a florescent-lit room running the width of the building, and it was about eight feet across. There was a desk with a cradle phone on it, a file cabinet, two chairs, and a cloth-covered couch under the framed picture of an old cargo plane. In the corner beyond the desk was a table with a two-way radio and microphone. Opposite the door that I had entered was a second open door which led to the hangar.

As I entered the hangar, I turned toward the wide, partially open door leading out to the landing strip. There were a number of bodies lying on the ground outside the door since we had no body bags. Inside the door were about a dozen or so wounded being cared for by several women. Some of the wounded were lying on blankets, but most were on the floor. I thought that we were fortunate if these were all the injured we had.

I stopped one of the women, told her I was a doctor, and asked her what she needed.

"Everything," she said. "Except for a few vials of morphine and syringes we have nothing. We've dressed the wounds with antibiotic cream and a few bandages and are offering what comfort we can along with our prayers. There's little you or anyone can do. I guess most of the medical supplies were left in the clinics."

The Marines had brought their medical supplies with them, but they consisted of some Demerol, syringes, a few antibiotics, and some bandages. I had brought the morphine, which the clinic didn't need, but we had no IV fluid or blood. There was little else to be done except to get them out of here.

"Do you know a Dorothy Roberts and where she might be?" I asked the woman.

"No, I'm afraid I don't; but if she's among the sick or

wounded, she's most likely in this area," she replied and left to tend a wounded Russian soldier.

As I walked among the wounded looking for Dorothy, I could see that there was little for me to do. Everything that could be done had been done, and medical expertise was of little help here.

I found Dorothy lying on a blanket just inside the door and stooped down next to her. I touched her face and asked how she was doing.

"All right, I guess," she replied. "My leg hurts only a little and I'm lucky to be alive. It could be worse."

Her voice was weak, but at least she was alive.

"Don't worry," I told her. "The planes are on the way and should be here in a few minutes. You were brave to try to help that soldier."

"I saw him fall and was near him. I just went without thinking about it. I wasn't afraid so I can't claim bravery."

"Well, you were brave, and you will be on the first plane out of here. Hang in there because you have a lot of life to live. You have to find that right man, marry him, and raise a family," I told her.

"Your plan seems to have worked, Robert. You've saved all of our lives. I had no idea when we met yesterday afternoon that you would be such a hero."

"I'm certainly not a hero. I just had an idea. Everyone else made it work, and I'm as surprised as you are about my part in all this. I would have laughed if you had told me yesterday that I was going to be a colonel."

She smiled at me and closed her eyes.

I stood and as I turned to go someone called to me. I looked around and saw Mary a few feet away lying on the floor wrapped in a blanket. She was very pale and looked like a doll in her blanket and wool hat. I went over and knelt beside her.

"Mary," I said. "What happened?"

"Colonel," she said in almost a whisper. "Our truck was hit by many bullets when we went through the camp. Henry was killed when he tried to protect me, but I was wounded also. Our truck was able to keep going. I think Henry died immediately because he never spoke to me again. Someone pulled him off of me when the shooting stopped. He bled on me, but I couldn't tell his blood from mine. He saved me."

"Please call me Robert," I answered. "How are you now? Have they taken care of you? Where are you wounded?"

"They gave me some shots and wrapped me in this blanket. I'm sure they did what they could. I think that I was shot twice in the side of my abdomen. It doesn't hurt as much now, but I'm so cold."

"I'm sorry, Mary. Is there anything I can do for you?"

"I'm cold. Is there another blanket? I know we don't have much."

"Let me see what I can find," I replied.

I looked around, but there were no unused blankets or jackets available. Then I noticed the dead bodies outside the door. Some of them had jackets or coats which they no longer needed. I went over to the bodies and found a Russian soldier with a long heavy coat. Although there was blood on the back and several small holes, Mary would not notice. As I lifted the body to remove the coat, the woman I had spoken to earlier came over to help me.

"I'm Robert Jacoby," I told her. "Are you familiar with that woman?"

"You already told me, Dr. Jacoby. I'm Sister Mary Alice and worked as a nurse at the missionary clinic. I looked at Mary's wounds and bandaged them. She probably has some internal bleeding as her pulse is rapid, she's hypotensive, and her abdomen is tight. I gave her a small dose of Demerol to ease her pain, and I hope that it won't drop her blood pressure further."

"I anticipate that we'll be out of here soon, and she can get medical help. I appreciate what you're doing, Sister. Take whatever is needed from the dead."

"We have been doing that," she replied.

It was difficult to remove the coat as the body was heavy. After we had wrestled the coat free, we carried it back to Mary and covered her.

"Thank you," she said and gave me a thin smile.

"You're welcome. You hang in there. The planes will be here in a few minutes, and you'll be on the first one out of here. It should be warm on the plane."

I touched her face, and then walked back to the bodies outside the hangar. There had not been time to arrange them or to treat them with the respect they deserved. That would come later. I looked through the dozen or so corpses that were piled there until I found Henry Jackson.

I looked down at him with sadness and thought how close I felt to him even though we had met less than a day ago. Shared danger makes friends quickly. I would miss him.

As I stood over Henry's remains, Sergeant Davis ran up to me and said "Colonel, the planes are less than two minutes out. The first will land and turn around, and then the second one will come in. The last plane will wait until the first two have left before landing. We're ready to load everyone."

"All right. What's happening on the road, and did you locate a fuel truck?" I asked. I thought we would need at least twenty or thirty minutes to get everyone out.

"Lieutenant Anderson reports that the first of the rear guard has engaged a force of ten or twelve trucks. Two were destroyed, and the other trucks have discharged their troops. Our men have pulled back to their second position, and the fighting is intense. Anderson doesn't expect the skirmishers will be able to hold out for long. They're in danger of being overrun by the larger force. They'll have to withdraw across the bridge shortly. They have one truck for all of them, but it's not far to the bridge."

"What about the fuel truck?" I asked again.

"Yes, sir," he said, and pointed to a truck along the side of the road. "There's one truck, and it's about three-fourths full. We're spreading fuel along this side of the road and in the grass along with several packages of C-4 and detonators. Although some of it will be absorbed in the ground, it will make a nice fire in the dry grass, and we'll be able to set it off remotely. We have also put C-4 and detonators along both sides of the road as well as in the middle. The engineers had a warehouse full of the stuff, and they brought it all with them."

"No point in leaving it for the rebels," I told him. "Is that a plane just off the distant end of the runway?"

"I believe it is, sir," he replied.

A moment later amid the deafening roar of jet engines the plane was on the runway and braking rapidly. It pulled off the runway in front of the hangar as the second plane landed. Both planes throttled their engines back and turned around in the small space available.

The sounds of fighting increased down the road and flashes of fire could be seen from where we stood. It was apparent that we would not be able to hold out for long.

The trucks were driven out to the first plane immediately, and the civilians were rushed on board. A group of men were helping to carry the injured from the hangar to the first plane. Everyone felt the urgency.

"Start loading the other plane with military," I ordered Sergeant Davis.

"Yes, sir. We're loading the bodies now and all spare men will get on as soon as it is finished. Do you want to board one of these planes?"

"No, I'll leave on the last plane."

There was an explosion followed by three more in the distance. The small arms fire increased again along with more small explosions, but except for the roar of the jet engines all was quiet or drowned out by the roar. We were sheltered from the jet noise by the building, but the quiet was relative.

Then there were several shots from nearby followed by screams and confusion among the passengers loading the plane nearest the road. As I looked toward the road, a group of soldiers ran into the woods on the opposite side and began firing.

"What's happening?" I asked.

After a moment Sergeant Davis said, "I think that a

few rebels were in the woods and fired on the planes, but they'll be killed. I don't know where they came from and can't tell if the shots hit anyone on the plane. Lieutenant Anderson reports that there are more rebels on our side of the river, and he's blown the bridge. He also says more of the rebel force have arrived at the bridge. He's used the one mortar he has to destroy the road and a few of the enemy trucks, but the river is fordable in some places. The enemy is being held at the bridge but is spreading along the opposite bank and may be able to ford beyond our lines. He doesn't think he'll be able to hold them for long."

"How soon will the planes be ready to leave, Sergeant?" I asked.

"The first plane should be loaded in the next few minutes. The second will hold more men than are presently at the airport."

"As soon as the first plane is out of here, see if we can land the last plane and load it while the second takes off," I told him. "Tell Anderson to begin withdrawing his men. Put the first of those on the plane until it is full. We can't afford to overload the last plane as the runway requires a short takeoff."

I knew that the planes were capable of short takeoffs, but I wasn't sure if they could with a heavy load. The first two planes would have the best chance of getting away safely, but there was little margin for error.

I left Sergeant Davis to carry out the orders and walked toward the corner of the hangar to see how the loading of the planes was going. Lily Blackthorne came running around the building and almost ran me down.

"What's wrong?" I asked.

"Some stupid kid is missing and his mother is having a fit," she said breathing heavily.

"How old is the kid?"

"I don't know. Seven or eight I guess."

"Well, I haven't seen him around here. Maybe he went into the hangar. Is the plane loaded?"

"Just about," she replied.

"Put the mother and her son on the next plane. And you get on the first plane, and that is an order. Understand?"

"Sure, but I have to find the kid."

"Then all of you get on the second plane."

Lily shrugged and walked into the hangar, and I walked back to Sergeant Davis to urge him to get the plane off as soon as possible, although I knew that was being done. He nodded and then said, "I've spoken to Commander Robertson, who's flying the last plane. He'll land as soon as the first plane has left. He'll clear the runway so that the other plane can take off. By the way, I don't believe that anyone was hit by shots fired at the plane."

"I'm happy about that," I said.

"Lieutenant Anderson is sending the first of his force back, and we can load them on the second plane. He'll hold out at the bridge for as long as he can and then join the few men we have guarding the road at the end of the runway. All of the bodies have been loaded, and...wait a moment, sir."

He spoke to the Marine next to him then turned back to me.

"The first plane is ready to leave, sir. He asks permission to take off."

"Clear the area behind him. Permission is granted."

"The area is clear," Sergeant Davis said, and relayed the order to the Marine next to him.

The deafening sound of the jet engine increased. I could not see the plane but pictured it pulling on to the runway, revving to full power, and then sweeping down the strip between the truck lights. A moment later it appeared down the runway and took off into the night sky. It almost seemed to metamorph into the last plane coming in, which landed quickly and disappeared behind the hangar.

Time seemed suspended as we waited for the troops holding the bridge to get to the airport. Finally I sat down in the front seat of the jeep to wait. Sounds of fighting could still be heard in the distance as we sat in silence.

Finally Sergeant Davis came over and told me that the first group from the bridge was approaching the airport and should be here in a couple of minutes.

"Has everyone been boarded who can be boarded?" I asked.

"Yes, sir," Sergeant Davis said. "Lily found the lost kid in the hangar, and she, the kid, and his mother are on board. All other nonessential personnel are on the plane except for Roger Taylor, who said he had permission to be on the last plane. There's still room on board, and we're waiting for Lieutenant Anderson's men to arrive."

"All right. Have Lieutenant Anderson evacuate the rest of his troops from the bridge if he's not done so already. Tell Taylor to send his story and to get on the plane. Get the second plane in the air ASAP and bring the defense back to the airport when the plane has left."

"Sir, we should keep the airport defense out until the last plane is loaded. If the enemy has not gotten here, there will be no rush; but if they are here, we can hold them until the last minute while we get the plane loaded," he suggested.

"Do it," I told him.

"We might want to get on board now, Colonel. We can communicate with everyone from the cockpit or through the small phones, and it will save time. The radio won't be necessary on board and can be left behind."

"Will you be able to ride in the jeep?"

"If we get rid of the radio, we'll all fit."

"Let's move," I said, and Jonsey threw the radio out as Sergeant Davis climbed in. Jonsey moved over to make room for him.

As we went around the side of the building, the noise of the jet engine hit us even though the engine was throttled back. Two trucks arrived at the same time we did. The men in them quickly boarded the plane, and we followed closely. The vehicles were driven out of the way of the plane, and the drivers joined us. Once we were inside the plane, the noise became bearable.

I made my way to the cockpit to introduce myself to Commander Robertson. He was a young man with blond hair and intense blue eyes and appeared as if he should have been in high school dating cheerleaders. His co-pilot, Mark Harrison, was in his twenties with brown hair and eyes. Both looked at me intently when I entered.

"Colonel Jacoby, I presume," Robertson said.

"Correct," I replied, and turned to Sergeant Davis to inquire where our troops were.

"All of the bridge force is pulling back to the airport and should be here in minutes," he told me. "The enemy is still mostly across the river and has no vehicles on this side when they do cross. If we hurry, we might be able to leave before they arrive. Also for your information Jake Alvoid was wounded boarding the plane."

"I'm sorry to hear that," I replied remembering the little boy who hadn't wanted to go to the bathroom before boarding the truck. "Is he hurt seriously?"

"I don't know any details, but I'll try to learn more later," Sergeant Davis said.

"The other plane is almost full, Colonel," Commander Robertson interjected.

"All right," I said to Sergeant Davis. "Get all of Anderson's men loaded and get that plane in the air. Are all the personnel from the trucks along the runway on board?"

"Yes, sir," Davis said.

"Then have the men guarding the road and end of the strip come back here as soon as the second plane is gone."

"Do you have any cover for us if the rebels get here before we can leave?" asked Commander Robertson.

"Yes, the road is mined, and we've poured aviation fuel along this side of the road. That will make a nice smokescreen when lit," I replied. "But with luck we'll be gone by the time their soldiers arrive."

"Your words to God's ear," commented Commander Robertson.

# Chapter Twenty-Four

Janet and Joy discussed neighborhood events while Jack listened and made occasional comments. They were carefully ignoring the hippopotamus in the middle of the room. Finally Joy asked Jack what he thought about Robert's situation.

"I don't know anything about Uzbekistan, Joy. I don't even know where it is on the map, and I am a salesman not a military expert. My ideas aren't worth much," he said.

"I know, but you must have an opinion. As for experts there are plenty of them on television, and they all have different ideas, which range from there's no problem to it's a disaster. You've known Robert for awhile and must have some impressions of him."

"I can't say that I ever remember discussing military tactics with him, but I always thought he was an intelligent man. I suspect there's a good reason why he was made a colonel and put in charge, and I think the government knows the reason but isn't saying."

"Then why did the State Department call to ask me to influence him to surrender?" asked Joy. "They could have just not put him in command."

"I don't know, but I guess the government is protecting itself politically," Jack replied. "I'm sorry but the situation appears gloomy, and there are no military options from our standpoint."

"Jack!" Janet said. "We're here to help Joy not add to her burden."

"She asked, and I gave her my opinion," he said defensively.

"It's all right," Joy replied. "I wanted an idea from someone who knows Robert. It's just so weird. I've been married to Robert for ten years and would never have expected him to be made an officer in the military unless it was the medical corps."

"It's after eight thirty and must be about four thirty there," Janet said. "Do you think there might be more news now?"

"It's five thirty tomorrow morning there, but it won't be daylight yet. Besides, it will take awhile for any news to get here after it happens there. But we can turn on the TV if you like," Joy said.

"Well, we can get another twenty different opinions from the experts," Janet commented.

Joy picked up the remote and turned on the television.

CNN was having another panel of military experts and journalists discussing the situation for the thousandth time. It was at least a big event for the news networks.

Sharon Lister was interviewing Mark Nevin, an aide to Senator Morris.

"Have you had any change in your views since we spoke this morning?" she asked.

"Not really," he answered. "Nothing's changed since then. I think the chance of the Westerners being freed is good if General Stratiscof keeps his promise. It would be to his advantage to do so. On the other hand it was not advantageous for him to have allowed or ordered the execution of the earlier group as they were not a threat to him. The situation there is unstable to say the least. We'll need to wait and see what develops."

"Our other guest is Doctor James Rothenburg from the Department of Russian Affairs at Georgetown University," Sharon said. "Can you add anything to Mr. Nevin's comments, Doctor?"

"I'm less optimistic than Mr. Nevin, Sharon. If General Stratiscof was not interested in this group, why bring his army to trap them? His military objective must be to join the rebel force facing the Russian Army. This whole operation is delaying that, and it makes no sense. I believe that the general is not in control of his men. It's the only explanation that makes sense. But then you have to ask why the president believes him."

"If I may interrupt, Sharon," Mark Nevin said. "There may be no available military force to attempt a rescue. After all, it would take a large operation to fight twenty thousand troops even if we had control of the air and used missiles.It also takes time to plan a rescue, and there was no warning that this was going to happen. The president may have no alternative other than to accept General Stratiscof's word. That would explain a number of things."

"If that's the case, Dr. Rothenberg, the outlook for the Westerners is rather poor, isn't it?" Sharon asked. "There are twenty thousand rebels facing three hundred in the refugee group, and the group that was killed this afternoon was much larger than this one."

"I'm afraid so, but we don't know what Colonel Jacoby has planned. There is some reason that he was put in command," Dr. Rothenberg answered.

"Wait a minute, Doctor. We're getting some new information," Sharon said. Joy sat back in her chair and stared at the television. Unless they were attacked early, it was too soon to expect any news, she thought. There was tightness around her heart, and she could barely breathe.

Janet reached across the table and took Joy's hand. They waited.

Finally after what seemed an eternity, Sharon turned her attention back to the camera.

"The details aren't available, but our reporter, Roger Taylor, has sent a message that the trapped refugees have broken out of the valley and are at the airport about five miles away. However, they're being pursued," Sharon reported. "Apparently one plane with refugees has taken off safely, and the second and third planes are loading. We expect more details in a few minutes."

"What about casualties?" Joy asked the television. "What about Robert Jacoby?" She got no response.

Sharon had gone back to the interviews. "As you

were saying, Dr Rothenburg, Colonel Jacoby seems to have had some ideas of this own. What do you think has happened?"

"I'm not sure how he accomplished it, but Colonel Jacoby seems to have gotten the refugees out. We must presume that this was the reason he was put in command."

"Mr. Nevin, do you have any further thoughts?" Sharon asked.

"It appears to me, Sharon, that if Dr. Jacoby or the Pentagon had a plan, it would not have been necessary to put him in charge. Lieutenant Anderson or Major Arinski could have initiated the plan without involving Dr. Jacoby. There is something that we don't know. As I think about it, if this were a government plan, it would not involve Dr. Jacoby at all; and if that is the case, then this plan is Dr. Jacoby's, and the government would not approve it."

"Sharon," said Dr. Rothenburg, "I don't agree completely with Mr. Nevin's analysis. The attack called for surprise, and that may have been the reason that the government was not notified or was notified but made no comment. Exactly what Dr. Jacoby's role was in all this is certainly puzzling."

"Thank you both for your comments. To reiterate, we have learned that the refugees are out of the trap set by the rebels and are at a small local airport. They're being evacuated by three planes and one of these is in the air safely. The other planes are still on the ground. The rebel forces are in pursuit, but we don't know whether the last planes are under attack. There have been both military and civilian casualties, but the number is unknown. Colonel Jacoby is still in command and is on the ground at the airport. We'll bring you updates as soon as we have them."

Joy felt the tears slowly run down her cheeks. Robert was all right even if still in danger. He would come home. She knew it.

# Chapter Twenty-Five

Looking out the cockpit window I could see a stream of trucks and other vehicles driving onto the field next to us and discharging men beside the two planes. The drivers abandoned the vehicles in an unorganized mass outside the hangar and ran to board the planes. Then the last of the men came only to our plane.

"The other plane reports it's full and requests permission to take off," Lieutenant Commander Mark Harrison said to me.

"Get them out of here," I replied.

The second plane's engine roared enough to be heard in our cockpit, and it turned in front of us heading toward the runway. At the head of the strip it headed down the runway immediately, and I watched as it lifted off into the night sky. At least we had gotten two planes away.

The plane had barely disappeared when there were flashes from weapons along the road at the opposite end of the airport. I had a sinking feeling in my stomach for the first time tonight. Somehow the rebels had crossed the river and caught up to us, but it made no sense. Why did they want to get us so badly? This couldn't be about torture and rape. They wanted to kill us for some reason. Did they just hate us that much, and if so why?

Sergeant Davis returned to the cockpit as another truck unloaded personnel next to our plane. Everyone was running, and the truck driver had to be told to get his vehicle out of the way.

"What's happening? Are all of our men withdrawing?" I asked Davis quickly. "How many men are left to board? I presume that the enemy has reached the end of the field."

"Yes, sir. They've gotten some of their trucks over the river," he replied. "There are about a dozen men in our rear guard. Everyone else is aboard except for Roger Taylor, but the last of the men are under fire from a small enemy force with more coming to join them."

I took a deep breath and tried to calm myself.

"Get our rear guard back here now," I ordered. "Set up a force to cover their withdrawal along this side of the field next to the plane, but make it a small detail. Tell Roger to send his story and get on."

"It's done, sir. As soon as our men have passed, we can set off the C-4 along the road. That should slow them down. Do you want to set the gas off now?"

"Not yet. We'll use it to cover our takeoff, but we need everyone on board now."

"Jonsey, get the rear guard back and loaded now," Sergeant Davis said into his microphone. "Set up the two grenade launchers and some automatic rifles next to the plane to protect their retreat. If the rebels follow them on the road, blow the mines once our men have passed. And get the journalist on board."

A few minutes passed as I watched men organize a line of defense to the left of the plane. There were continued flashes in the dark off the other end of the runway indicating ongoing fighting, and in the east the sky was brightening above the mountains. Dawn was approaching.

"Colonel," Commander Robertson said. "Ground fighting stinks. Let's get in the air where we'll have a chance at least."

"All fighting stinks," I replied. "I am a damn doctor, and not even a military one at that. I don't like any of this. That's what we have you military types for, and I am glad of it. We appreciate your risking your life to come for us."

"That's what I get paid the big bucks for," he said with a smile. "I know that you don't want to leave any of your men behind if you can help it, but remember the ones we have on board already."

"It's a long-standing Marine tradition to leave no one behind, and I think everyone understands it," I said. "It's been my tradition for about twelve hours now."

"Yes, sir. I understand. I hope that your smokescreen works for us."

There was firing off our left wing, and several explosions along the road followed by a mass of blasts about two-thirds of the way down the road as the C-4 was set off in that area. A moment later a truck swung in behind us, stopped next to the hangar, and six men jumped out heading for our plane.

"Are those the last of the rear guard?" I asked Sergeant Davis.

"Is that all of them, Jonsey?" Sergeant Davis asked into his microphone and waited for a reply.

There was a soft noise outside of the plane. We were taking automatic weapons fire, but it was not from large caliber weapons. We were lucky. There was an immediate return of fire from our defenders followed by more C-4 explosions.

"Except for the defensive detail everyone is aboard, sir," Davis told me. "Roger has sent his story and is on with his equipment."

I didn't need to tell him to get them all on quickly.

"Colonel," Lieutenant Commander Harrison said, "get strapped into that seat. As soon as the rear door is closed and latched, we'll roll and blast out of here with everything we have."

I sat down, placed my backpack under the seat, and buckled the belt as I told Sergeant Davis, "Get them on the plane and set off the aviation fuel and whatever else you can. Get everyone buckled in including yourself."

Before he could relay the order, the plane rocked as there was a flash along the road followed by dust and smoke. There were more explosions when the fuel alongside the road was ignited. Although the sound of the explosions was muffled in the roar of the jet engine, the plane didn't move. I could see the last of the defense force and the men outside the wing of the plane sprinting toward us. Again time seemed to stand still, but at least there was no enemy fire. After an eternity Commander Robertson said something into his microphone, and the plane began to move slowly forward.

The fire beside the road burned brightly and illuminated the whole scene in an eerie flickering light. Although the fire and smoke obscured the road and the hills behind it, the runway was clear and partially lighted by the fire. Even the headlights of the vehicles along the runway were dimmed by the brightness of the blaze, but the sky to our right was clear with its stream of stars.

The plane turned onto the runway, and suddenly I was pushed back hard against the seat and could barely breathe as the plane leapt forward under full power. Even in the cockpit the roar of the engine drowned out all thoughts. Alongside the runway the trucks' headlights flashed by in a blur like streetlights seen through a wet car window. We have a chance, I thought, if no one in the field beyond the end of the runway is waiting for us with a shoulder-held rocket launcher.

# Chapter Twenty-Six

Janet came around the table and put her arm around Joy's shoulders.

"Robert is all right. They've escaped the trap, and he is probably on the plane now and safe. It's a miracle, but they are safe," Janet told Joy.

"I know," Joy said, "but it's so hard to believe. I mean all of it. Robert being trapped and made a colonel and the escape is like a dream, not real life. These things don't happen in my life. I'm an ordinary housewife and mother. My husband is a doctor, not a colonel in the Marines. We're ordinary people."

"Sometimes ordinary people are put in extraordinary situations," Janet replied.

"Maybe, but not us," Joy said.

The phone rang, and Joy told Janet and Jack to let it ring. It was a reporter wanting to talk to Joy and asking her to speak to him. This was followed by another and another call, all from reporters wanting to interview Joy. Soon Joy knew they would begin showing up at her house, and she asked Jack what she should do about that.

"I think you can get police protection under these circumstances," he said. "The media will be here in droves, and I must say that I'm surprised they aren't here already. We'll never be able to call out on your line. Let me go to our house and call for you."

"Thanks, Jack," Joy replied.

The phone continued to ring. How many reporters are there? Joy wondered. Then there was a familiar voice. It was her sister, and Joy picked up.

"Hi, Martha," Joy said.

"Joy," Martha said. "Who have you been talking to? Mother and I have been trying to reach you for the last hour. Have you heard the news about Robert?"

"Yes, I have heard. I haven't been talking to anyone, but everyone in the world has called. It's mostly reporters wanting to know about Robert, and I don't know anything. I'm as much in the dark as everyone else."

"You haven't heard anything from him?" Martha asked.

"No, nothing. What I know is from the news, same as you."

"So you still don't know if he's all right. When did you last hear from him?"

"It was several days ago. There's probably something wrong with his cell phone or he would have contacted me when this all started. Don't worry, Martha, my neighbors, Janet and Jack, are with me, and Bobby is asleep. I'm fine."

"All right, but you let me know if I can do anything. Mother and I just wanted to let you know that we love you."

"Thank you, Martha. I love you too."

Joy hung up the phone and looked up at Jack, who had come back during her conversation with Martha.

"There are already two patrolmen on the street," he told her. "They'll send more if they're needed. TV crews are beginning to arrive and will be kept off your property. You will have to speak to them sooner or later, but I did meet a William Arthur, who said he spoke to you earlier today. He's outside and asked if you would see him."

"All right," Joy said. "But I won't speak to anyone else until I know that Robert is safe."

Jack went back out to let William Arthur in. Joy pushed at her hair and wondered if her makeup looked all right. She had presumed that she would have a chance to freshen up if she was going to be on TV, as she was still wearing the blue dress from this morning and had not retouched her makeup since before leaving for the store.

Jack returned with a cameraman and a man that Joy presumed was William Arthur. He was an attractive man with classic features but was smaller than Joy had imagined. He wore a tweed jacket, white shirt, plain brown tie, and brown wool pants with brown shoes. He came directly to her, extended his hand, and introduced himself and his cameraman.

"I'm William Arthur, and this is Cal Barber. I appreciate your seeing us. I know this has been a busy day for you and that you're being hounded by the media, of which I am one," he said with a nice smile.

"I'm Joy Jacoby,"she said. "I don't know why everyone wants to speak to me. I've had no contact with my husband since this began and have no information about what's going on except what you already know. There's nothing new that I can tell you."

"I know. I would like a brief interview about why your husband is in Uzbekistan, and if you have any thoughts as to why he was selected to lead the military in this refugee group. Since this will all be over shortly, I would hope you would speak to us again afterward. I will be as little trouble as possible, I promise."

Joy saw the small figure of her son dressed in his superman pajamas come into the room behind Cal Barber. Joy stood and went to pick him up.

"What are you doing awake?" she asked him.

"I heard all the noise and it woke me up. Who are these people, Mommy? Is that a real TV camera? Did something happen to Daddy?"

"No, I think Daddy is fine. These two men are from CNN about Daddy being made a colonel, and you know Jack and Janet."

Janet came over and took Bobby from Joy. "Let's you and me go upstairs, and I'll tuck you in bed while your Mommy talks to these nice men. What do you say?"

"I want to watch Mommy on television," Bobby protested.

"You can see your Mommy on television tomorrow,

honey," Janet told him. "I think there's a little hot chocolate left if you would like some."

"Okay, I guess," Bobby agreed, and Janet took him
and the carafe of hot chocolate upstairs.

Joy turned back to William Arthur and said, "I'll grant
you a brief interview, but I wish to be alone when Robert
calls. I especially don't want you telling me on camera
that Robert is dead."

"That's a harsh criticism, although it may not be en-
tirely unjustified for some in my profession. I'm sorry that
you feel that we would intrude at a time like that, and I
promise I won't. That's not the way I work. Besides, if
something happens to your husband, our reporter will
be lost with him since they're together. All of us want
them to get out safely. If you want to be cynical about it,
the bigger story is if they make it, not if they're lost."

"I am sorry, but this is very difficult for me," Joy
replied.

"I understand. While we're setting up here why don't
you take a few minutes to compose yourself and to
change clothes? There's no hurry. We will wait until you
are ready."

Joy left the kitchen. She would check on Janet and
Bobby and redo her makeup. Maybe this interview
would take away some of the stress of worrying about
Robert. He was alive, out of the trap, and safe at the
airport. She should feel better about that, although for
some reason she didn't. She wanted him safe at home
with her.

# Chapter Twenty-Seven

Three-fourths of the way down the runway the plane lifted off the ground and headed straight up, keeping me pinned to my seat. I felt as if my heart and stomach were going to come up into my mouth. Finally we turned right and began to level off and slow down to the speed of light. I could breathe again. Out the cockpit window I could see a mass of stars and nothing else. We had made it. No one had shot us down, and as near as I could tell, there had been no shots at us at all. Of course, once Commander Robertson had turned on the jets, I doubt if I would have noticed anything less than the end of the world.

"It seems as if we're away safely, Colonel. There are

no warning lights indicating we are being pursued by missiles," Robertson said.

"Did we sustain any damage back on the ground?" I asked.

"We were hit by small arms fire, but nothing critical seems to have been damaged. I used a lot of fuel on the takeoff, but the tanks don't seem to be leaking. We should have enough fuel to get us home if we are careful. We were lucky. Setting the gas fire to mask our takeoff was a great idea because without that we would have been a sitting duck for anyone on the road."

"Mining the road helped also. That must have surprised them. May I go back to talk to my men? I have no idea what happened back there," I told him.

"Yes, sir. The rest of the flight should be smooth."

I took off my safety strap and went to look for Lieutenant Anderson. I wanted to learn how his part of the attack had gone. He was in the rear of the plane talking to several Marines who were being administered to by a corpsman. I didn't see much blood, although they were in obvious pain. The corpsman was using bandages and medicine from his field kit.

"How bad is it?" I asked.

"There are a couple of broken bones that occurred during the takeoff when they weren't in their seats and were thrown against the rear of the plane, sir," the corpsman replied.

"We got through the whole fight to break a bone in the plane. How can that be?" one of the Marines asked.

"Life is stranger than fiction," I replied and turned to Lieutenant Anderson. "Lieutenant, would you fill me in on your part of the operation?" I asked him. "The convoy got out so you did a great job."

"Thank you, sir. It went very well. Actually it went better than I had expected. The advance party moved across the river and took out the guards, who were either asleep or smoking and not paying any attention. They were not expecting us to attack. My troops went first, and then the group to take the hill and bring down the climbers followed. As you know, the night was dark, and we encountered no one on our way up between the camps. The advance group quietly took out several enemy soldiers they found wandering around. No alarm was raised. When we joined the advance group at the top of the hill, all was well. It was like an evening stroll. The Russians came behind us and went off to the left behind the camp."

"Didn't you have some of the Russian troops with you?"

"Yes, sir. Most of my force was Russian. I had all the English-speaking men and many who didn't. I put two or three Russians with each Marine and formed groups of ten or twelve men with their own assignments. We moved behind the camps, which required us to go fairly far up the hill and delayed us a bit. I sent two of the Marines to meet you and to take out the guards at the hut, and twelve men to clear the road up at the main junction. The rest of us moved down to the road where we split up into those who would attack the rebel force from the rear and those who would clear the road to allow the convoy to pass. There was a huge number of enemy men spread across the road, the slope, and the opposite side of the river. This group was alert except for a few asleep in the rear of the camp. I presume the latter were to take over the next watch. It was fortunate that we didn't arrive at the change of the watch.

"All of my men knew where to go as we'd worked it out before hand. It took a few minutes to get everyone into position, and I didn't know how long it would take the other force to get to the top of the hill or for you to arrive at the hut. I allowed ten minutes for my men to get into position and then ordered the attack. It was interesting that no one, even the trained troops in front of us, noticed us. I think you were right, sir. They didn't think we would attack.

"After ten minutes we began the attack. They were taken completely by surprise. We killed all the enemy troops near the road and in the rear including those who were asleep and several of the mortar crews without the loss of any of our men. We just walked into their trenches and fox holes and gunned them down. We then occupied the trenches as defensive positions, and I sent two men to lead the convoy through. They told me that they flashed their light and in less than a minute they heard the trucks begin to move. A minute later the first of the convoy came through. There was some firing on the convoy, but we silenced that as quickly as possible. I'm sorry I didn't have the road completely safe. I hope that no one was hurt.

"Once the convoy had passed completely, we began to withdraw. The men on the road got on the trucks at the end of the convoy and were followed by those along the road edge. I sent up a flare to signal the rest of my men to pull back to the road where I had planned to set up a rear guard until the Russians got off the mountain. In the middle of all this the mortar from the mountain helped considerably to keep the enemy off balance. Also as you predicted, we had no trouble with the enemy to our left. They were completely involved in fighting in the other direction.

"We set up our rear guard and received little opposition. Up to that point we had lost no one and had only three wounded. Unfortunately, one of those was serious, and he died later. We were able to bring his body out on one of the trucks. The rear guard had no formal line, but we formed a defensive position behind the enemy encampment. The convoy was just a few yards ahead of us and was waiting for the Russians from the hill top. Later I learned that the first of the convoy with the civilians had gone on. I stayed on the road and brought all of my men to this side of the river. There was no effort by the enemy to attack us, and we kept silent. After about ten minutes you and the Russians arrived, and we loaded into the trucks. I thought we would run into the enemy on the main road, but, as you know, we got to the bridge before they came after us. If they had met us where we turned on the main road, we would have been in big trouble."

"Was there a problem getting everyone into the trucks at the end of the convoy?" I asked him.

"It was pretty crowded. The Russians took the first few vehicles, and we filled up the rest. A number of the vehicles were lost at the end of the convoy crossing the river. The drivers escaped, abandoned their vehicles, and got into the last of the trucks that made it across the river. I don't think we lost any of the drivers. However, there were plenty of rebel trucks alongside the road, and we took six of those. We also found an old tank, which we used as a road block after the convoy left. All our vehicles were being driven by civilians, which was great."

"OK. Fill me in briefly about the defense at the bridge."

"That also went well, but we couldn't hold them for long. The engineers or whoever planted the explosives saved the day. After you went through, I sent a group of the Russian soldiers, who'd been guarding the road junction, about a half mile up the road to warn us of approaching enemy troops and to slow them down. It didn't take long for the rebels to arrive. I doubt if the Russians had time to set up much of a defense before they arrived. Our men fired on the rebels and knocked out the first two trucks, which blocked the road, and they killed or wounded most of the troops in the vehicles. Then they withdrew to their trucks and came back to the bridge to join us.

"Fortunately the bridge had already been mined because I hardly had time to put our men on either side of our end of the bridge before we were under attack. I really couldn't organize any sort of defense in the few minutes I had, and I left it to the noncoms to do what they could. I did get the trucks out of sight of the attackers as these were our means of escape. I didn't have time to do anything else.

"When the enemy arrived, they stopped short of the bridge. I had planned to blow up the bridge with the rebels on it, but they were too smart for that. We used our rocket launcher to hit the first truck when it stopped, and it blocked the road. I ordered everyone to open fire on the rebel troops, and we blew up the bridge. Only our end of the bridge collapsed, but it was enough to keep them from driving across. As more of the enemy arrived, they spread along the opposite bank of the river and soon outflanked us. I recognized that we couldn't hold out long and notified you. I was afraid that the rebels would cross the river above and below us and catch us in a cross fire. We held for a few minutes, and then withdrew to our trucks under covering fire from our rear guard. We returned to the airport where we were told to board the planes. I think we lost two men and four others were wounded. We got all of our force on the planes including the dead."

"As I said, you did an outstanding job. I need to report to the admiral what you've told me."

I went forward and asked Commander Robertson if he could put me in touch with Admiral Clark. When I spoke to the admiral, I told him in some detail about the operation but could not tell him about the Russian attack on the mortars on the hilltop as that group was not on our plane. I did mention the papers that I had picked up from the hut where General Stratiscof had made his headquarters, but I told him that I had not read them and didn't know if they were of any importance. I did not tell him about the finger. He said there would be a debriefing after we arrived. It would all be put together then. I was sure that would include how I was elected to take control, but that wasn't my concern now.

I then asked if I could be patched through to my wife to whom I had not spoken for several days and was told that would be no problem. RHIP (Rank Has Its Privileges). I gave them the phone number.

# Chapter Twenty-Eight

When Joy came back downstairs, the camera and lights had been set up in the kitchen and were centered on the kitchen table with two chairs behind it. Joy glanced out the front window as she walked toward the kitchen and noted that the street was filled with trucks and people. There were several policemen standing on the sidewalk in front of her yard, keeping the reporters and people at bay.

She came into the kitchen, noticed the message light on the answering machine blinking, and went over and deleted the messages without listening to any of them. There were fewer calls now, but she wanted the answering machine to continue to screen all of them. She only wanted to speak to Robert. He had been her life since they had been married, but she hadn't realized how much of her life revolved around him until now. Of course she loved Bobby, who was an intricate part of her life, but Bobby was also a part of both their lives.

Joy sat at the table, and Jack bought her a cup of coffee that he had brewed while she had been upstairs. She tasted it, and it was excellent.

"May we begin?" asked William Arthur.

"Yes," Joy said and set her cup down.

An assistant attached a microphone to Joy's collar. Then the lights came on and were blinding until her eyes adjusted to them. She tried to compose herself as William took the seat next to her.

"Mrs. Jacoby," William began. "Tell us a little about yourself. How long have you been married, where did you grow up, and where did you and Robert meet?"

"Robert and I met in Boston while he was in medical school, and we've been married about ten years. We have a son, Bobby, who's eight years old. I grew up in a town along the coast just north of Boston. After I graduated from high school, I went to college in Boston and worked as a secretary after Robert and I were married."

"Would you tell us about Robert?"

"Robert was born in Charlottesville, Virginia, and moved a good deal as a child. His father was a school teacher and enjoyed living in different areas of the country including Seattle where Robert spent most of his time as a child. After graduating from high school he went to the University of Washington but decided to come east for his medical school training and was accepted at Tufts Medical School."

"Did he spend any time in the military?"

"Yes. After college he was in the army for two years. I'm not sure what he did, but he was never in combat and was not an officer."

"So you know of no reason from his background that would explain why he was made an officer and put in command of troops?"

"No, I don't, except that he's a very bright man and would do whatever was necessary to get everyone out safely. But even if he had an idea about how to escape, I don't know why he would be put in command."

"When did you last hear from him?"

"It's been several days. He was still at the clinic when I spoke to him last. He hoped they wouldn't be bothered by the rebellion as they were in a small, unimportant town."

The phone behind Joy rang again, and she ignored it. The answering machine picked up after the third ring. "Mrs. Jacoby, this is Seaman Simpson. Would you answer if you are home? Your husband would like to speak to you."

Joy was out of her chair before he had finished speaking and grabbed the phone. "Robert, are you there?"

"Just a moment, ma'am," came the reply.

"Joy, is that you?"

"O God, Robert! Yes, I'm here," Joy said through her tears.

The lights from the TV camera went dark and the camera was turned off on a signal from William Arthur. As he had promised, he would not intrude on this moment.

"I'm so sorry that I haven't called you, but my cell phone gave out, and it's been crazy here," Robert said. "I'm all right and on a plane back to a carrier. I love you and am sorry I couldn't call sooner."

"I love you too, and I miss you and want you home."

"I miss you too and will be home as soon as I can. I didn't realize how dangerous missionary work could be. I can't talk longer now but will call you again as soon as I get the chance."

"Good-bye, Robert. Hurry home to us. We're waiting."

"Good-bye, honey."

Joy sank back in her chair and cried with relief.

# Chapter Twenty-Nine

After speaking to Joy I felt much better, and I looked out at the dark sky. We were flying away from the dawn, and it would not be light for an hour or more. I knew that we were flying fast, but looking at the stars we could have been standing still. The cockpit was illuminated by the instrument panel lights, and I could only see the backs of the pilot and copilot. There had been little conversation since I spoke to Joy using the headset that I had on.

"Are we going to the carrier now, Commander Robertson?" I asked. I realized that I had no plans beyond getting on this plane, and having accomplished that I should feel relieved and tired. I wasn't tired, but I thought that would come after the excitement wore off.

"Yes, Colonel. It's the nearest base, and we should be there in a couple of hours. You can grab a nap if you want. After we land, you'll get a chance to clean up and eat, but probably they will want to debrief you before you go to sleep."

"How long does the debriefing last?"

"For you, I don't know, but it could take awhile."

"I have some experience with fatigue. Like the military, medicine requires many sleepless nights, although neither profession is helped by tired personnel."

"You have that right, Colonel, but it goes on anyway," he replied.

I wondered what could take so long about my debriefing. My part in the operation had not taken much, and my information came from other people who were available for questioning. My biggest problem might be convincing them that not surrendering was the best approach considering that the president had ordered the surrender. It could be argued that any deaths that had occurred were my responsibility as with surrender they would not have happened. I had no doubt that we would have all been killed as the convoy ahead of us had been, but would others agree? Even if they did agree, would politics prevent them from saying so? The president had ordered the surrender. How would he react to these events? Sometimes facts were not as important as perceptions, and the public believed what they were told.

If I was held politically responsible for this operation, could I protect those who had helped me? Sergeant Davis and Major Arinski would be all right, but what about Lieutenant Anderson and particularly Admiral Clark, who had risked his career by appointing me a colonel, an appointment that I wasn't sure was legal? I might be able to protect them by showing I had forced Anderson and Clark to agree to my demands. I would have to await the debriefing and see how things went, but if blame was to be placed, I was responsible.

"What is Admiral Clark like?" I asked Commander Robertson.

"He's a good man. Does what he believes is right and stands behind his decisions and his men. He's well respected among the crew. He's a graduate of Annapolis, served in Vietnam, and rose through the ranks because of his ability rather than influence. Don't worry. He'll stand behind you, and he has support in Washington. I don't know what support, but he has influence in Congress as well as at the Pentagon. Of course, who knows about politics? It may destroy all of us yet."

"You seem to have some political insight," I replied.

"Yeah, my father was very interested in politics and was involved at the local level in the Republican Party. Politics was always a subject at the dinner table, and I am well aware of how it works."

"I hope your rise to commander wasn't political, or should I ask Mark about his flying ability?"

"I don't think my father carried enough influence to help my military career," he laughed. "But you needn't worry. Mark is an excellent pilot."

"Since you have some political insight, how do you think our attack and escape from Stratiscof is going to play in Washington?" I asked him.

"With all the publicity I think you'll be seen as a hero

rescuing doomed women and children from certain death from villains. No one expected you to be able to get away from twenty thousand armed troops, but you did somehow. The president will have to devise an explanation of his order to surrender that will be palatable to the public, and he'll have to do it without admitting the military was unable to carry out the rescue. You can expect a ceremonial welcome with a parade and pictures with all the bigwigs."

"Wonderful!" I said. "I want to get back to my family and life. Instead I'll be expected to make speeches, probably a lot of speeches. What am I going to say? What I need is a speech writer. Public speaking is not my forte."

"You should have thought of all that before saving everyone and becoming a hero," he replied. "After all it's better than being charged with disobeying orders and causing the dearth of innocent people or being killed yourself."

"If you say so," I said, but I decided to keep the finger removed at the hut as my ace in the hole and put it in my pocket. I decided to pass on all the other papers and items.

# Chapter Thirty

After a few minutes Joy straightened up, accepted a tissue from Jack, turned to Arthur Williams, and said, "I guess you would like to continue the interview now that I have some news."

"Yes, but you can take time to fix your makeup again. I have already told our studio about the phone call. They're not happy about having no film, but they'll get over it."

"I appreciate your turning off the camera and certainly owe you an interview for that. It will only take a moment to repair my face, and I'll be ready to go."

"Take your time, but hurry," Arthur said with a smile. "In the meantime let's see what the channel has on,

Jack. I'm sure it will be about the attack. They must be scrambling for experts to interview since there are no pictures from the event."

As Joy left the room to go upstairs, Jack turned on the TV. It turned out that Arthur was wrong. There were pictures taken by Roger Taylor being shown, and when that was finished, a pretty dark-haired woman asked her guest to comment on them.

"That's Carol Mims," Arthur said. "I don't know who is with her, but we'll supersede them once we get this interview going. I think it will be in real time."

"It's hard to tell much from the film because it was dark and obviously shot without lights," the guest said. "I think you'll need the photographer to describe the action in order to have any understanding of the events. This is true for almost any real action film shot at night as the camera angles are not ideal as they would be in a directed film.

"However," he continued, "let me comment on what we know. Somehow Dr. Jacoby has led a vastly outnumbered group of Marines, Russian soldiers, and a few civilians including women and children out of an impossible situation. All day we've been hearing about the anticipated massacre and how there was no escape without massive military intervention, which would not be available in time, and yet despite that he got them out. I think this is a fascinating story, and he must be a remarkable man. He isn't John Wayne, Superman, or Rocky, but an ordinary American placed in an extraordinary position and accomplishing a miracle. It's a miracle when three hundred or so people defeat twenty thousand armed troops to escape entrapment. I'm sure there will be explanations of how this was done, but, although I am not especially religious, in my opinion it's a miracle accomplished by a few military people led by your average American hero. If we lived in biblical times, it would be recorded in the religious history."

"Thank you for your commentary," Carol said. "That was Lieutenant General Joseph Bernard, United States Army, retired. After a short break we'll return with more on this fast-breaking story including an interview with Mrs. Jacoby. Stay with us."

Joy returned looking refreshed and confident. She sat down at the table, and told Arthur Williams she was ready when he was.

"It will be a minute or so," he replied. "We'll follow this break and will be live. Just relax and be yourself."

"If Robert can defeat thousands of armed troops, I should be able to do a live interview without trouble," Joy said.

"Absolutely!" Arthur said as he reached over and turned off the television set, and Cal Barber clipped the microphone back onto Joy's blouse.

After a few moments the television lights were turned on and Arthur said, "Carol, I'm here with Mrs. Jacoby, who spoke to her husband a few minutes ago."

Then turning to Joy, Arthur said, "Mrs. Jacoby, I know this has been a trying time for you and your family and that you must be relieved to learn that your husband is all right. Would you tell us what he said?"

"As you know, it was a brief conversation. He apologized for not calling sooner but said that his phone was not working and that he'd been rather busy."

"I bet he has. Did he give you any details of the past

few days?"

"No, but now that I know he is safe, I can wait to learn the details."

"I know that you told us earlier, but would you tell us again about where you grew up and how you met Robert?"

Joy repeated what she had told Arthur earlier. She would talk all night if they wanted. Robert was safe, and everything was fine.

# Chapter Thirty-One

After several hours of cramped flying, we landed on the aircraft carrier *Eisenhower* in the Arabian Sea. There had not been much space to move around in the plane, particularly with the number of people on board, and when we landed, I was stiff and in need of a restroom, or I guess "head" would be the appropriate term on board a vessel. I was allowed to freshen up before being taken to meet Admiral Clark, but I kept my backpack with me. I had strapped it on before we left the plane, and I kept it on despite offers from various naval personnel to carry it for me.

I met Admiral Clark in his office. He was about six feet tall, balding, and had a pleasant smile when he returned my salute and greeted me. He was clean shaven and did not appear to have been up all night, although I am sure that he didn't sleep much awaiting news about us.

In contrast I was wearing my dirty jacket, pants, and boots. I had washed my face, combed my hair and shaved, and taken off the bulletproof vest. Otherwise, I looked exhausted and as if I had been walking through the woods all night.

He extended his hand and said, "I've been looking forward to meeting you, Colonel. It's not every man who stands up to a Marine officer and takes on the problems of the world."

"I didn't realize I was taking on the world's problems. I thought I was saving my own neck," I replied as I shook his hand.

"That may be, but you took on some political as well as military problems when you escaped. Some of the political problems are still around and will need to be dealt with. Please sit. I won't keep you long as I know you are tired and hungry. You'll have to be debriefed before you get to sleep, but I think we can arrange breakfast first."

I sat in the chair in front of his desk and said, "Let me start by thanking you for putting your career on the line for us. No matter what anyone may think, we felt that we would be killed if we surrendered. If you had not agreed to put me in charge, it would have made a bad situation much more difficult. You played a large part in our success."

"I really had no choice. I agreed with you that your best chance to escape alive was not to surrender, but my orders were to tell you to surrender. That brings us to this morning's problem. You are now a Marine colonel who has disobeyed an order in the face of the enemy. On the other hand you avoided a difficult situation for the administration and the Pentagon, who probably agreed that all of you would have been murdered if you had surrendered. Now what are we going to do about the situation?"

"I presume you're going to tell me, sir," I replied.

"You did this operation on your own and deserve full credit for your success, but we need to let Washington off the hook. It's not politic to rub the government's nose in its past mistakes. I can't order you to lie, but we need to agree on an approach to defuse the situation. Your length of service has been brief, so please talk to me as a civilian."

"Have I been discharged already?"

"No" he laughed, "but you think more like a civilian, and I need your help. We're in this together even though neither of us wanted to be here."

"Yes, sir. I think the best thing to do is to let the public think that the government knew about the plan beforehand or at least knew there was a plan. I don't care if I get credit for the idea, but if this strategy had come from Washington, there would have been no need for me to take charge. Besides, everyone in our group knows it was my idea, and it would be difficult to keep that from the press. Actually, Roger Taylor has sent a report to CNN already."

"Do you know what was in the report?"

"No, but we must presume he sent all the information that he had."

"What exactly are you suggesting?" he asked.

"I think that I'm suggesting that we imply that Washington knew there was a plan, even if they didn't know what the plan was. They approved of our taking the action that we felt was best since we were there and since the less talk there was about the attack the less likely it was to reach General Stratiscof. That was what you did. Why couldn't Washington have done the same?"

"Good plan! It should satisfy everyone or at least most everyone. I will contact the Pentagon and tell them that's what you will say. They can take it from there."

"Admiral, I won't be lying because, if I'm asked what Washington knew, I can safely say I don't know what you relayed to them. It should work, and I don't have to remember what to say."

"You are a hero to the American people, and I don't think that the Pentagon will want to hold a court-martial for your disobeying orders. Besides, if the people at the top are able to get some of the credit, they'll be happy. I like working with you, Colonel. You know how to get things done."

"Thank you, sir. May I ask one more thing? I would like to visit my wounded as soon as possible, and with the others who were with us and lost family members. I would also like the opportunity to write to all the families of the military and civilian casualties, and I'll need their addresses."

"Of course. You will remain in command of both the Marines and the Russian force until you or they depart. Major Arinski and Lieutenant Anderson will take care of the day to day activities, but you'll remain the commanding officer. I will also arrange for a proper uniform for you. I hope that we have one in the ship's supply room. I expect the press will come aboard as soon as they can, and we want you dressed appropriately."

"Thank you, sir. What do I do now?"

"Intelligence will debrief you in an hour. In the meantime you may stay here and order whatever you like for breakfast. I have duties to attend to. After the debriefing you may visit the sickbay. They would probably like to check you anyway."

After debriefing by intelligence I would like a nice nap, I thought.

# Chapter Thirty-Two

I found that I was hungry and ate an excellent breakfast of scrambled eggs, crisp bacon, toast, coffee, and
orange juice. Either food aboard ship was good or I
was starving or both. At any rate I felt much better after
eating.

As soon as I was finished a seaman took me to a
small room with a table and six chairs. A young female
seaman was seated before a recorder. One of the other
chairs was occupied by a stocky older man with sparse
brown hair and tanned features. He was dressed in a
light tan jacket, white sport shirt, and light green pants.
Sitting next to him was a young naval officer with blond
hair and pleasant features and dressed in white shirt,

pants, and shoes.

The officer stood, saluted, and said, "Welcome, Colonel. I'm Captain Peterson from naval intelligence, and this is Mr. Lambert. Please have a seat. I hope your breakfast was satisfactory."

"It was fine," I replied. I sat in one of the chairs across from Peterson placing my backpack on the floor next to my chair.

"We know that you're tired after your ordeal and will make this as brief as possible," Captain Peterson began. "We want to learn what took place yesterday afternoon and last night. There may be things of importance that you would not think to tell us, and therefore we may ask questions. Often details can be important. Why don't you begin by telling us what happened, and then we can go back over it in detail."

I could see that this was not going to be a brief interview.

"It might be well to explain Colonel Jacoby's situation to him before he begins," Mr. Lambert interjected.

"Might I have a cup of coffee while Mr. Lambert is explaining my situation?" I asked.

"Of course," Captain Peterson said and went to a small table that was behind him. He poured a mug of coffee and slid it across the table to me after asking if I wanted cream or sugar.

Mr. Lambert looked annoyed but waited until Captain Peterson had resumed his seat before speaking.

"You realize that when you accepted this temporary commission as a Marine officer, you became subject to military law. Your first action was to disobey an order from the president, the commander in chief. You decided not to surrender as ordered but to attack a rebel force in their country after they had promised to free you in the morning. This decision caused the unnecessary deaths of several military and civilian personnel. You could face court-martial and be sentenced to a military prison. Your best course of action now is to be fully cooperative."

Although I had planned to be fully cooperative, Mr. Lambert's approach made me angry. I am an American citizen and should be entitled to certain rights. I was not the terrorist here and had not murdered American civilians and military the day before. However, this was not the time or place to bring up any of that. It was also apparent that Mr. Lambert was a CIA interrogator or a civilian employed for that purpose. I needed to control my temper and answer any questions briefly and to the point.

"Thank you for your explanation, Mr. Lambert. Shall I begin now?" I asked Captain Peterson.

"Yes, please."

I spent the next fifteen minutes telling my story of the events. I knew that they would be interviewing Lieutenant Anderson, probably Sergeant Davis and some of the civilians. I didn't know if they would include Major Arinski. I tried to be as accurate as possible and at the same time succinct.

"What made you think you were qualified to take command?" asked Mr. Lambert. "You have no experience in command, and there were two military officers there."

"Lieutenant Anderson was going to turn us over to the people who had slaughtered the group ahead of us, and that would have led to our deaths as well," I replied. "Major Arinski was not in a position to take control of American troops and would have taken his soldiers into the mountains last night. Having seen what happened to the group ahead of us few people wanted to surrender. On the decision to fight or surrender the camp was divided including the Marines. Since no one was taking control, I offered to lead and was approved by the civilians and later the officers, even though I have no significant military expertise."

"What gave you the right to decide to fight when the president had negotiated a surrender?" demanded Mr. Lambert.

"It was clear to us what would happen if we surrendered. It would not have been pleasant. The one thing we could agree on was that. A leader was needed, and I agreed to lead."

"I think this is a matter that can be dealt with later if need be," said Captain Peterson. "Let us move on. Why did you think this plan would work?"

"The division in the enemy camp was obvious just by looking at it; and if we weren't going to surrender, there were not many choices left. Both Lieutenant Anderson and Major Arinski thought this was our best chance. I think most of the Marines agreed. Besides, no one felt we had a chance in an attack, including General Stratiscof. The enemy was unprepared for an attack and would be taken by surprise as turned out to be the case."

"In the hut what made you think the wounded man was Stratiscof?" asked Mr. Lambert. "He could have been any officer."

"He said so," I replied.

"What about the other man? Who was he? It must have occurred to you that he was of importance," he said.

"There were no introductions, and I don't know who he was. He could have been an officer, but I don't think so."

"Why don't you think so, and if you thought he was important, why didn't you bring him out?" asked Mr. Lambert.

"We discussed world affairs briefly, which would not have been of particular interest to an officer. As to bringing him out, I had three hundred and some people to worry about getting out. He was not a priority and, under the circumstances, it would have been very difficult to bring out a prisoner," I replied.

"Maybe your priorities were wrong. He might have provided information that would save thousands of lives," Mr. Lambert said.

"Maybe he would have provided nothing. I was not going to risk any lives taking a prisoner. If he was important, he's dead now."

"And of little help to us," he replied. "As a military officer your first concern is what is best for your country and then what is best for your troops."

"Let me point out that my commission was to rescue the personnel under my command, which included women and children, and it was not to gather information. Besides, if we had surrendered, you would not have this man, whoever he may have been. I have the impression that you are disappointed that we survived."

"No, Colonel. I'm glad you got out, but it could be an

embarrassment to our country that you didn't surrender as ordered."

"Really, Mr. Lambert. The embarrassment is that fifteen hundred Americans were brutally murdered, and yet our government came back to 'negotiate' with the killers. Speaking of embarrassing how embarrassed would the government be if we had surrendered as ordered and been killed?"

"I don't think that would have happened," Mr. Lambert said.

"You are right, Mr. Lambert. You weren't there, and you don't think."

"Let us move on," Captain Peterson interjected. "You killed Stratiscof and this other man because you didn't want them to organize any pursuit, but you were pursued anyway; why?"

"I don't know," I said. "I think they felt they had been attacked and were responding."

"Your contention is that they were out to murder and rape. If that were the case, they would not have gone after you once they had been attacked," Mr. Lambert said.

"These were Stratiscof's trained troops, and not the tribesmen who were most likely involved in the massacre. At this time I think the troops were responding to our attack."

"Could you identify the weapons that their troops had?" asked Captain Peterson.

"They had a conglomeration of weapons from rifles to mortars and automatic weapons and rocket launchers. However, that would probably be a better question for the military that was there."

Questions went on for another hour. I provided what information I could. At the end Mr. Lambert said, "This incident may be perceived as an unprovoked attack for which you are responsible, and you may have to be charged."

"I doubt that, Mr. Lambert." I replied. "It was more provoked than our attack on Iraq."

"That may be. I'm just saying that I would watch my step if I were you."

After Mr. Lambert had left, I gave the papers from my backpack to Captain Peterson.

"Why didn't you give them to us earlier?" he asked.

"Because I don't know who Mr. Lambert is," I replied. "I think that he's either CIA or an employee working for the CIA. If he's the latter there are very few if any rules applying to him, and I don't approve of use of these contracts. I hope that you will not pass these papers on to him until you know what is in them."

"Don't worry," he laughed. "I would be crucified if I did that. May I inquire if you have anything else of interest?"

"No, you may not ask, but I would like to ask a favor. I would like to visit my wounded."

"Of course, Colonel. Would you follow me, please?"

He led me through a maze of corridors and decks to the sick bay and introduced me to Seaman Mary Cruiz, who was helping to care for the wounded. I asked her about Mary, Dorothy, and Jake Alvoid.

She told me that Dorothy was in surgery, and they thought she would be all right. She had been shot in her left leg, and the bullet was lodged next to the bone. The surgeon expected her to make a full recovery after the bullet was removed.

Mary was in recovery, but she had lost a good deal of blood. Jake was in a ward, and his mother was with him. He had been shot in the shoulder, which broke two bones, and he had lost a fair amount of blood. The bones had been set, and he was being transfused. He would require more surgery, but he was expected to make a full recovery. They planned to move both Mary and Jake to a military hospital in Germany or the United States as soon as the patients were stable.

When I went to Jake's bed, I found both his mother and Lily Blackthorne with him. Somehow I was not surprised to find Lily there.

"How is he?" I asked Jake's mother.

"He's asleep, but they say he should be fine," she replied. "I can't believe he was shot. We were almost safely on the plane. Why him? He's just a little boy."

"I don't know, but I'm glad that you are all right and that he'll be well. You should get some rest so that you can be with him when he wakes up. They'll probably keep him sedated for awhile."

"I'm going to rest nearby so they can call me when he wakes."

When I left, Lily went with me. I asked her what her plans were after she got home.

"I don't really know at this point. A few hours ago I wouldn't have given us much of a chance for a future. Now I guess I'll return to Delaware where I still have a beach house and figure it out from there. I think I might try to find work a little closer to home where there's less excitement."

"I'm sure you will be successful in whatever you try," I

told her. "You're a remarkable woman. I'm glad to have known you. Meeting you and some of the other people has been one of the positive things to come out of this experience. Without your help and support we would not have escaped. I can't thank you enough. I hope you'll come to Maine sometime and meet my wife. I'll tell her about you."

"Thank you, Robert, but it was your leadership that got us out. I did little. When it came to the bottom line, it was your courage to stand up to and win over everyone including the civilians and the military that made the difference. We all owe our lives to you. I will not forget you."

"I just pointed everyone in the right direction and got out of the way," I said. "You organized and encouraged the civilians, most of whom were too afraid to do anything. Thank you again and please come to visit me if you can."

She turned and hugged me, and we said good-bye.

# Chapter Thirty-Three

I slept the rest of the day and missed lunch. I was awakened by my orderly late in the afternoon and given underclothes, socks, shoes, and a Marine officer's uniform complete with eagle insignias. It would appear that the ship was fully stocked for all events.

As I was dressing, Captain Peterson dropped by to see me.

"I thought you might like company for dinner in the officer's mess," he said. "It would also be an opportunity to discuss the papers you provided me this morning."

"That would be great," I told him. "Besides, I don't know where the officer's dining area is."

"Not to worry. You have an aide assigned to you. He

got your uniform and will see to all your needs. I've told him that I would take you to dinner."

"What a life," I said with a smile. "Tell me about the papers."

"The papers are largely in English and are from the legation. Fortunately all the sensitive papers were probably destroyed before the staff left. The other items are in Arabic, and we've translated them. They dealt mostly with Stratiscof's intentions and operations. There were no surprises there. There was one paper that dealt with Al Qaida and seemed to be suggesting there was a link between Stratiscof and the terrorist organization. You said that you took these from the hut which was Stratiscof's command center."

"Yes. Are you thinking that the man with Stratiscof may have been a terrorist?" I asked.

"That's a possibility. You said that you didn't recognize the man."

"No, but I'm not sure I would have recognized bin Laden much less any of his people. I would be happy to look at any photographs of terrorists you may have. I might be able to pick him out."

"I was coming to that. We have quite a few photos for you to look at. Do you know if Major Arinski is familiar with any of the terrorists?"

"I have no idea. You would have to ask him," I replied. "After all I only met him last night, and we've been quite busy since then."

"Well, you can become better acquainted tonight. I took the liberty of asking Major Arinski and Lieutenant Anderson to join us for dinner. After dinner we can look at some of the photos. Sorry this is not a luxury cruise.

We do have to work. They also said that you might have something else of interest."

"Yes, I do. I had been keeping that in reserve in case I needed it during my defense."

Peterson laughed and said "Not to worry. Admiral Clark told me to tell you that you're a hero. He said you would understand. As for Mr. Lambert, he was recalled to Washington and will be leaving this evening."

"All right!" I exclaimed. "Let's eat. I'm starving."

I was sure my cabin was secure, but I took the finger with me anyway.

After dinner Captain Peterson led me back to the conference room we had used earlier. I took one of the seats, and Captain Peterson got coffee from the side table and brought two mugs to our table.

As he sat he said, "I'm afraid that I may have been a bit premature in saying that you were free of Mr. Lambert. I was told during dinner that he wanted another interview with you before he leaves. He probably learned about the papers you gave me and wants to ask about them. I had reported them to our office in order to have them translated, and the CIA was informed. I'm sure that he's not happy with either of us."

Mr. Lambert entered then, placed his bag on the floor next to a chair, and put his briefcase on the table. Peterson was right. He was not happy. I wondered if he was ever happy.

"I'm disappointed," Mr. Lambert said to me. "You withheld information from me when we spoke earlier. I know that you don't like me, but you should not have let your personal feelings interfere with giving information when you were debriefed."

"I did not withhold information. I answered all your questions as accurately as I could," I replied.

"You didn't provide the papers that you took or the finger you cut off one of the men in the hut. I learned about them from other interviews. I don't consider that being cooperative."

"You didn't ask about any papers or anything else that I gathered. I gave the papers to Captain Peterson as he's in the military for which I work at the moment. You are an unknown. You never said who you are or what your interest in this event was. I presume you work for the American government, but so do a great many people who have no need to know about what I know. I see you as a prosecuting attorney wanting to put me in prison. Why would I provide you with anything? I knew you would learn about everything from other interviews, but I was not going to help you since you gave me the impression you were here to prosecute me."

"I'm sorry you feel that way. We're working for the same side. I would have thought you would know that. I'm trying to do my job, which is to gather information that might protect our country from terrorist attacks. If you're offended, I'm sorry."

I looked at him for a moment and then told him, "Despite what you may think, I'm not the enemy. I am a doctor who was trying to help in a foreign country. Like everyone else in our group, I was caught in a threatening situation not of our making. Our only objective was to get out alive. Even the military that was there was trying to escape, not gather information for you. You have said that you were glad we escaped, but I have the impression that you think we should have surrendered even if we died. We had no ulterior motives. We just wanted to get out alive and did what we thought was best to accomplish that end. I'm sorry that you feel differently. My personal opinion is that we did what was best, not only for us, but for our country. If we had surrendered and been killed, which is what would have happened, it would have been a big embarrassment to the president and therefore to our country."

"That may or may not be the case," Lambert said. "I'm only interested in information, and you are not providing it."

"You have all that I had except for the finger, which is of dubious value. I took the finger as I thought it might tell us who he was, but whether he was important or not is unknown. I kept it because I felt I might need it in my defense and was not sure you would provide it."

"You don't seem to trust your government."

"The government is made up of many people and groups, not all of which I trust. The president's decision for us to surrender, we believe, would have led to our deaths, and this belief was confirmed by General Stratiscof before he died. I think the president saw no other alternative. If I am to be court-martialed for not surrendering, as you suggested, I would need whatever evidence I have. I know that you were trying to intimidate me with the threat of a trial, but it was a possibility. Since I am told now by reliable sources that a trial is unlikely, you may have the finger."

"Thank you, Colonel," Lambert said as he picked up the severed finger from the table where I had placed it. "This will be useful even if it isn't from one of the well known terrorists. It may identify the groups with which

General Stratiscof was in contact."

"From what little he said I suspect that he might be someone of significance."

"Why do you think that?" Captain Peterson asked.

"He implied that his death would not hurt the cause, which suggests he was important in the movement. He also said that he had expected to have been killed earlier. That seemed to me to indicate he was of some importance."

"It will take time, but there are ways of identifying the person to whom this finger belonged," Mr. Lambert said. He did not elaborate.

"Do you need anything else for now?" I asked.

"No," Mr. Lambert said, "but Captain Peterson will want to talk to you further after we have analyzed what we have so far. My flight is waiting, but I may see you back in Washington."

I was sure that I would repeat my tale of the events several more times before I got to Washington and that I would be in Washington for some time before I got home.

"All of you will be leaving in the next day or so," Captain Peterson told me. "The Russians will be departing tomorrow afternoon as their government is sending two planes for them. The civilians will depart tomorrow afternoon also and will be going to Rome by navy transport and then fly commercial airlines to New York. I'm not sure when you and the Marines will leave, but Admiral Clark thought you might like to address all of your command tomorrow morning on deck. It will be like a parade formation with the band, press, and all available personnel."

"My farewell speech to the troops, so to speak. Yes, I would like that, and I'll need to work on my speech tonight. Could I meet with Major Arinski before the formation?"

"I think that can be arranged. Would you want anyone else there?"

"Yes, Lieutenant Anderson, Sergeant Davis, and John Branson. They, along with Lily Blackthorne, to whom I have already spoken, made up the officers of my command. I would like to thank them personally."

"I can arrange that for the morning. The parade gathering will be at eleven hundred hours and should last about an hour. It is partly for the press which will arrive earlier. Any particular music you would like to request for your introduction? You know the president has 'Hail to the Chief'. Maybe you would like something like that?"

"I doubt that 'Hail to the Chief' would be appropriate. How about Copeland's 'Fanfare to the Common Man'?"

"I'll see if the band knows that one, but you're hardly the common man, particularly now," he said.

"The public didn't know or care about me two days ago, and I'm the same man as I was then," I replied.

I am very much the common man, I thought, or at least I would like to be. Next I thought about what to say to people who had accomplished so much in saving our lives. Of course, I knew only a few of the civilians and even fewer of the military, but I had led them. They had put their trust in me, and they had changed my life. Even those I knew, I had known less than two days, and yet I felt closer to them than I did to some people

I had known all my life. How could I say good-bye to all of them? A few days ago we had been strangers and tomorrow we would go our separate ways, but for a brief period we had shared our lives, faced death, and survived. It was an experience that none of us would forget, and we would probably remember each other even if we never met again. What could I say to them?

# Chapter Thirty-Four

I rose early the next morning, shaved, and dressed in my new Marine uniform with the aid of my orderly, who made sure I was correctly attired for the coming occasion. Following breakfast I met with Major Arinski, Lieutenant Anderson, Sergeant Davis, Specialist Jones, and John Branson in the cabin where I had been debriefed. The military were in dress uniforms, even Major Arinski, although where he got a Russian major's uniform on such short notice I have no idea. All except John stood and saluted when I entered the room.

I returned the salute and asked them to be seated.

"I won't take much of your time as I know that you're preparing to depart today and we have the ceremony this morning, but I wanted to tell each of you how much I appreciate your efforts in freeing us. There's no question that our escape would not have succeeded without your cooperating with each other and bringing all the disparate groups together in a very short time. You worked as a unit with Americans under Russian command and vice versa. You cooperated for the greater good. Even the civilians worked together. I thank each of you."

Major Arinski stood and said, "The situation was desperate, but you offered us a chance, and we took it. As poor as the chance seemed, it was better than facing the mountains, and surrender was not an option. There was no choice but to work together. Besides, there was military pride. If we were going to die, we could do it fighting like men."

Lieutenant Anderson stood also and added, "The major is right. We all expected to be dead today, and we wanted to go out putting up a good fight. I admit that I didn't expect to be here today. That was the reason I was glad to have you take command, although I fought you for it. I didn't want to be responsible for all the deaths, and I didn't want it on my record that my last act was to surrender even though I was ordered to do so."

"I guess I didn't have a military record to worry about," I replied. "I just wanted to get us out and was foolish enough to think my plan might work."

"That was the thing, Robert," John said. "As far as the civilians were concerned, they needed to believe in a chance, and you believed and acted as if you believed. They were happy to follow you."

"All the military personnel felt that way," Sergeant Davis said. "You had a plan and acted on it. You provided leadership and didn't get in the way of our doing our jobs. They didn't have time to think about the odds or what might happen. They just wanted to do something."

"Well, I may have had a plan, but you made it work. I suppose most of you will receive orders telling you where to report next as will I. What about you, John? You have a choice."

"I don't know. I haven't had time to think about it," John replied. "As you requested, I'll accompany Henry's body back to Mississippi for burial. After that I guess I'll go home for awhile and then decide what to do. I will probably remain in the missionary field, but where I don't know. What about you, Robert? Will you go back to Maine to your practice?"

"That's what I would like to do. I want to see my family and return to my former life. I didn't know how good I had it. However, I have been ordered to Washington first and have to stay there for awhile before I can return home. I hope that my wife and son will be able to join me in Washington. I haven't seen them in several months."

"Maybe you can make the military a career," Lieutenant Anderson suggested.

"No, I'm a civilian at heart. I'll leave the adventuresome life to those of you more qualified for it. I plan to resign my commission before I'm asked to do it, and return to civilian life."

"Do you know when you'll be leaving?" John asked.

"I'm scheduled to go tomorrow morning. I don't know

why I'm not going with the rest of the civilians."

"That's easy," laughed Lieutenant Anderson. "You're military now and will leave when it's best for the service. I also suspect that the Marine Corps won't want you to resign. They like to keep their big names attached to the service. Who knows, maybe they'll retire you."

"You mean after my long and illustrious career?" I said.

We were interrupted then by the announcement that the formation would be in twenty minutes.

"It's been my pleasure to have met you, and I wish each of you the best and will see you on deck," I said, saluted, and shook hands with each of them.

After they left, I went to my cabin to pick up my address.

# Chapter Thirty-Five

The ceremony was to take place on a portion of the mammoth gray deck. There was a gentle breeze blowing just enough to make the microphones whistle occasionally and to keep the carrier island flags from drooping. It was a warm day with hazy sunshine and high clouds in sharp contrast to the cool, crisp, clear skies we had seen in the mountains of Uzbekistan. The sea was blue and mildly choppy, but the ship was perfectly stable. I didn't see any land.

I sat on the low stage with Admiral Clark and his officers. My Marines and Russian soldiers were standing in front of us, while the navy crew was behind them with the press and cameras in the rear on another low platform so that they had a clear view of us. The sea stretched out to the horizon behind them. The band was located to my right, and the civilians were behind them.

The ceremony had been brief so far. The band had played several pieces that I did not recognize, but music was not one of my strong points. The band played "Fanfare to the Common Man" after I was introduced. I was pleased that they knew it.

I stood and went to the microphone on the podium. I wasn't particularly nervous looking out over the people in front of me as I had some experience with public speaking from teaching medical students and other doctors at seminars. However, this was different. I was not teaching. I wanted to express my feelings about our common experience to those who had been there with me.

"Although I met you only a short time ago," I began, "I feel as if I have known you for a long time. Danger brings people together like no other experience, and I doubt if any of you would argue with me that we've been through a harrowing event in our lives. A week ago none of us would have predicted these events. We had come to a foreign land in peace to serve our nation and to offer our services to the people there. We came from many backgrounds and experiences and with different hopes and dreams, but we had in common our wish to improve the lives of the Uzbek people by bringing peace or knowledge or hope or health.

"These aspirations were interrupted by terrorists attempting to assert their will over the land and wishing to destroy us. They didn't wish us harm because we stood in their way since we didn't. They wished us harm because we were there, and they thought they could. In a horrible manner they destroyed the group of Westerners fleeing ahead of us. These were our friends, coworkers, and countrymen. Then the terrorists pursued us and trapped us in a valley from which there was no escape except through them.

"However, they miscalculated. You came together and refused to surrender. Everyone, both military and civilian, Russian and American, men and women and children, showed courage and a will to win in the face of overwhelming odds. I salute you. You have not only saved your own lives but have brought honor to yourselves by winning a victory like none the world has ever seen. Three hundred Spartans fought four thousand Persians at Thermopylae, but they were defeated in the end. You fought twenty thousand armed rebels and won. Although I will receive many of the accolades, it was a victory won by your determination and bravery.

"Personally it's been my honor to have been with you. I only know a few of you, and I regret that I didn't have the opportunity to meet each of you for you are remarkable people.

"I don't know what the future may bring, but whatever it may be, you should walk tall and be proud. You've earned it.

"I also want to acknowledge and thank Admiral Clark, Commander Robertson, and all those who risked their lives to rescue us. Without your aid, none of us would be here today. We owe our lives to you, and no words can adequately express our debt or gratitude.

"Now as I say good-bye, I pray that God may bless

and protect you and grant each of you a safe trip home. Thank you."

I returned to my seat and looked out over the heads of the gathering in front of me and over the blue sea and thought of my home so far away. I wondered what Joy and Bobby were doing. Since it was early morning in Maine, they were most likely asleep in their beds. I wished I was there also. It was one of the few times in my life when I felt lonely in a crowd.

# Chapter Thirty-Six

Joy looked out of the huge window that faced the landing field at Reagan Airport in Washington, D.C. Beyond the runways, which were active with planes landing and taking off, was the Potomac River, which she could not see. On the far bank she could see trees whose leaves had not yet begun to change to their fall splendor, and behind them was downtown Washington with the Washington Monument and in the distance the Capitol Building. The afternoon was clear and warm, and her view was unobstructed except for the planes.

She and Bobby were standing at the window while Mark Hanson, a Marine lieutenant who was their escort, found the gate at which Robert's plane would be landing. She thought it was strange that Robert, now a Marine colonel, was flying on a commercial airline and not landing at Andrew's Air Force Base, but she had not asked any questions. After all, the arrangements had been made for her and Bobby's transportation, room and board, and all their expenses had been paid. Their flight had been met by a limo with Mark in charge. They had been driven to the Shoreham Hotel on the edge of Rock Creek Park and had been settled into a suite overlooking the park. There were flowers and a fruit and cheese tray, which Bobby loved, and in general they were treated like royalty.

Last night they had eaten at the hotel and slept well. After breakfast this morning Mark had picked them up in the limousine and taken them on a tour of Washington. Bobby loved the limousine ride and stared out the window at the sights. They had gone past the Capitol Building, the Washington Monument, Jefferson Memorial, and the tidal basin with their only stop being at the Lincoln Memorial. After visiting the Lincoln Memorial and looking down at the reflecting pool, they went across the street to see the long black wall with all the names on it that was the Vietnam Memorial. They crossed in front of the Lincoln Memorial to view the cast iron figures making up a patrol in the Korean War Memorial.

They returned to the hotel for lunch and to bathe and change clothes. Even Bobby was impressed with his treatment and with the tour and cooperated with his bath and dressing. For him that was a change.

As she looked back over the past week, Joy thought how strange and in some ways exciting it had been.

Then she corrected herself. It had only been five days since Robert's escape from danger. After her interview and some pictures, the media had largely disappeared. There were still a few photographers around taking unexpected pictures of Bobby and her, but life had returned to normal. Bobby was a celebrity at school where everyone seemed to know about his father. Joy had tried to play this down with Bobby so that he wouldn't have such a big head, but she had not been totally successful. Of course there was Janet, who was elated at living next to an American hero's family and was constantly inviting Joy over to meet friends. Joy was polite but refused as many of these invitations as she could and tried to keep Janet and Bobby separated. As she reflected on it, maybe life had not returned to as normal as she had first thought.

She had spoken to Robert briefly every day. He said that he had been ordered to Washington and asked that she and Bobby meet him there. She had agreed and couldn't wait to see him and hold him, but before she could begin to make arrangements, she was contacted by someone form the State Department who told her that everything was arranged and that her tickets would be at the airport. All she had to do was pack clothes for herself and Bobby for about a week.

Now they were waiting for Robert's plane to land. She was dressed in the light gray dress with dark trim that Robert liked. She had on matching shoes, bag and hat. She wanted to look her best when Robert saw her. She had been warned that the press would be here in force to meet Robert, who was seen as a hero by the public. Although the press had interviewed Robert overseas, he continued to be a big story, and there had been something about him or the fight in Uzbekistan every day on television. So far the press had not found her at the airport, but that was about to change as they would be waiting at the gate where Robert would disembark from the plane.

Joy turned from the window and saw Mark hurrying toward her. He looked dashing in his Marine uniform, and she wondered if Robert would be in uniform. She had not thought about that before.

"Mrs. Jacoby, Robert's plane will be unloading down this way in a few minutes," Mark said. "I'm afraid the press is there already."

"We knew they would be here, Mark. We may as well face them now."

"Yes, ma'am. Please come this way. We need to hurry as the plane is early and has landed already. It should be at the gate in a few minutes."

Joy took Bobby's hand and followed Mark down the main concourse to their left. They passed several gates before Joy saw the crowd ahead of them. She tightened her grip on Bobby's hand as they moved toward the gate. The mass of reporters and camera crews parted as Mark pushed through them allowing her and Bobby to pass. A number of inane questions were shouted at her, and she ignored them.

Mark had cleared a spot to one side of the exit ramp for them, and she could see down the corridor where the passengers were unloading. Then suddenly she saw Robert, tall and attractive in his dress Marine uniform, and she felt the tears running down her cheeks ruining her carefully applied makeup. Bobby saw him

too and began pulling her toward him. How handsome
Robert looked, she thought, and then they were both in
his embrace as the cameras flashed around them.

254